Night Preacher

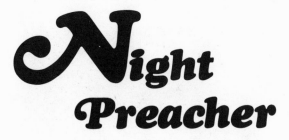

Night Preacher

By
Louise A.
Vernon

Illustrated by
Allan Eitzen

HERALD PRESS
Scottdale, Pennsylvania
Kitchener, Ontario

NIGHT PREACHER
Copyright © 1969 by Louise A. Vernon
Published by Herald Press, Scottdale, Pa. 15683
    Released simultaneously in Canada by Herald Press,
    Kitchener, Ont. N2G 4M5
Library of Congress Catalog Card Number: 73-94378
International Standard Book Number: 0-8361-1774-3
Printed in the United States of America
Design by Gary Gore

10 9 8

CONTENTS

1   THE FORBIDDEN NAME

ON market day Bettje woke at dawn and listened to the hum of people on their way to the marketplace in the heart of Amsterdam. She tiptoed from her pull-out bed, unlatched the upper half of the front door, and gazed at the busy street and boat-filled canal.

Two cows, prodded by their peasant owner, lumbered past the open door close enough for Bettje to touch. An immense longing welled up in her. Oh, to have a cow! Father had often told her and Jan, her brother, how he used to milk cows near Witmarsum when he was young. If only he would buy one!

The back door squeaked. Bettje heard her father welcome an early morning visitor into the study. She recognized the high, cracked voice of old Lukas Lambert and smiled. Father loved to talk, but when old Lukas chattered on and on, Father had to keep still out of politeness.

"Yes, Menno, you can thank Jan Claes for seeing that your books fall into the right hands," she heard the old man say. "Let me see—wasn't it six hundred copies he printed in Antwerp? At the meeting last night someone said two hundred have been sold in Holland already, most of them right here in Amsterdam. My nephew has one." The old man's voice softened with affection. "Carries it with him everywhere."

Bettje heard Father exclaim in dismay.

"Don't worry, Menno," old Lukas continued. "He didn't write his name on the flyleaf. If he thought the authorities were after him, he could always drop the book in a canal. Still, you know how rash these young people are—just daring the authorities. Sometimes I think the young ones act foolish on purpose just to prove themselves."

While Lukas continued to chatter in the other room, Bettje leaned over the door ledge to watch the boats go under the bridge. The thump of wooden shoes on cobblestones startled her. A young man fled past the door, his eyes wide, his short, hooded cloak billowing behind him. Two companions followed close behind.

"The bridge! The bridge!" one shouted. "Hide until we find you a boat!"

In swift sympathy Bettje clung to the door ledge. Should she call to the man? No, she dared not. Even though Father helped people every day and often at night, he had warned her and Jan never to tell anyone his name or where the family lived. Father's word was law. She could not disobey.

Bettje tiptoed to her mother's sickbed near the hearth fire. "Mother, it's market day. May Jan and I watch from the bridge?" Excitement gripped her. She and Jan had never gone out alone before. If only they could see the young man escape in a boat!

Mother raised her head. "Is the baby still asleep?"

Bettje peered into the wooden cradle. "Yes, Mother."

"I hear voices. Who is with your father?"

"Lukas Lambert."

Mother listened for a moment and pursed her lips. "I hope he doesn't talk like this to everyone. It is very dangerous—" She broke off. "Where is your brother?"

Bettje laughed and pointed to the upper pull-out bed. A leg and arm dangled over the edge. "He's asleep. But he won't mind if I wake him—not if we can go to the bridge. May we?"

Mother nodded with a sigh. "I just don't feel well at all. You and your brother get dressed and break your fast with some bread and cheese."

When Bettje and Jan were ready, Mother warned them, "Don't mention your father's name. Don't tell anyone where we live. This is more important than you can possibly realize. Will you remember?"

"Yes, Mother," Bettje and Jan replied.

Mother sank back on the bed and closed her eyes.

Once outside, Bettje and Jan hurried to the bridge to watch the latecomers on their way to market. A boatman for hire rowed past. The two men Bettje had seen earlier hailed him and beckoned to their friend huddled under the bridge. The boatman scratched his cap-covered head, but tied his boat fast and allowed the man to step in. With frantic haste, his friends tried to push the boat into midstream, but the rope held. Suddenly, the boatman stood up and shouted, "Anabaptist! Anabaptist! Here's an Anabaptist! Send for the beadles!"

The passersby took up the cry of "Anabaptist." People ran from their houses to watch. A constable came on the run, seized the young man, and tied his hands behind his back.

9

Horrified, Bettje clung to Jan's hand. If only she had called Father! Surely, he would have helped the young man escape the authorities—a word she had learned to dread from Father's whispered remarks to Mother when they thought she was out of earshot.

Two priests ran from a church across the canal and talked to the captive. The young man refused to answer, but stood with head bowed until the constable pushed him down the street.

The two priests started across the bridge. "We must rid the country of these accursed Anabaptists," one said.

"But have you noticed if you put down one, a hundred others take his place?" The other priest shook his head. "What mistaken courage these people have!"

At that moment a procession emerged from the church. Men in flowing robes carried crosses and sacraments on pillows. The passersby crossed themselves. Bettje watched in wonderment. Why were they making such odd gestures? Father never did. A heavy hand fell on her shoulder. She looked up into the round face of a priest.

"Here! You children know better than this. What do you mean standing like that without honoring the sacrament of our Lord?"

Bettje trembled. She had never been this close either to a priest or to a procession. Always before, Father had turned down a side street whenever they came to a church.

The priest gave her a little shake. "Well! Cross yourselves."

"I—I don't know how," Bettje murmured.

"What! This is an outrage," the priest thundered.

"Where do you live? Who are your parents?"

Bettje shrank back. The very thing Mother had warned them about had happened. She longed to be safe at home—anywhere except under the hands of this merciless questioner. Oh, if only she hadn't been so eager to come out alone with Jan! Her heartbeats hammered in her throat, but she determined not to tell Father's name, nor where the family lived, no, not even if they tied her hands behind her back. She would obey Father, no matter what happened.

With sudden calm, she looked up at the priest. A church bell clanged. The priest hesitated, muttered to his companion, and both hurried away.

On the way home, Bettje and Jan watched two children of the neighborhood, a boy and a girl, build a dike. Water from a recent rain had trickled over the edge of the canal.

"Why don't you help us instead of standing there?" the boy asked.

Delighted at having something to do, Bettje and her brother gathered handfuls of sand and grass sods for the dike.

"It's going to overflow," the boy shouted. Bettje worked even harder. Like everyone else, she knew about floods, the slow-creeping water that pushed, teased, and nudged its way sometimes to the very doorsteps.

"Wouter! Lavina!" a woman called from a nearby house. "Come home at once." The boy and girl did not move. The housewife ran out and flapped her apron at Bettje and Jan. "You horrid children! Don't you ever come near here again. Stay home where you belong. Better yet, leave the city before worse happens to you."

11

Bettje brushed sand from her fingers and stared at the woman. Had she gone out of her mind? What had happened?

"Don't stand there batting your eyes in all innocence. Your father put you up to this, I know. The whole neighborhood has heard about him. But he's not going to bring death or exile to my family."

In spite of Bettje's astonishment, she saw that the woman was really frightened.

"Go, both of you." The housewife's voice rose to a scream. She half carried, half pulled her children to the house, bolted the lower half of the door, then slammed the upper half shut. Bettje and Jan stood alone.

"Did we do something wrong?" Jan asked.

"No. Come on home. We didn't want to play with them, anyhow," Bettje said, but her thoughts whirled. What was Father doing that made people turn against his children?

"I wanted to finish the dike," Jan wailed.

"Well, we can't now."

"What did that woman mean? Did Father do something bad?"

"No, of course not. You know he's the kindest father in all of Amsterdam," Bettje assured him. After all, Jan was a year younger than she was. He couldn't be expected to understand as much as she could. She would have to find out what kind of work Father did. Always before, he had said he helped people. Then he would add, "When you children are older, I'll explain."

I'm older now, Bettje thought, and made a decision. *We'll stay and finish the dike. We haven't done anything wrong.*

As she and Jan worked, doors facing the narrow street would open an inch or two. Faces peered out. Then the doors closed. Once, a woman with two children tugging at her skirt came outside, shaded her eyes, and gaped at Bettje and Jan. Another time, Bettje glanced up and saw several women huddled together. An old man on crutches shook one crutch at them.

Bettje pounded dirt and sods into the dike, busy with her thoughts. Whatever made the neighbors act in this hateful way resulted because of Father. She knew Jan, too, understood the silent threats all around them.

"It's about Father, isn't it?" he whispered.

"Yes, but don't pay any attention to these people."

A little later, the mother of Wouter and Lavina, the two children who had started the dike, left her house and headed toward the marketplace. Wouter and Lavina came out again, with many furtive glances over their shoulders. They watched Bettje and Jan work on the dike.

"Let's help them, Lavina," Wouter urged.

"No. Mother told us we can't play with them," his sister said.

Bettje did not look up. "Why can't you play with us?"

"Because you're bad," Wouter said.

"But we like you," Lavina added. "If only you weren't going to burn for eternity, we could play with you, but you're wicked, wicked, wicked."

"What did we do?"

"It's not you, exactly. It's because of your father."

"Well, what did he do?" Bettje asked.

"He does awful things at night," Lavina said.

"What kind of things?"

"I don't know, but my mother said he was bad, and so are you."

"He's an Anabaptist, that's what he is," Wouter said.

Anabaptist! Like the runaway man that morning!

"Your father's name is so terrible, my mother doesn't even say it out loud. She whispers it, like this." Lavina cupped her mouth with her hand.

"Our father's name is not terrible," Bettje stormed. "Come on, Jan. We're going home."

At once Wouter started to chant, "Anabaptist! Anabaptist! Shame! Shame! Shame!"

Lavina echoed him, and Bettje and Jan ran toward home, the hateful words pounding in their ears.

Jan panted, "What's an Anabaptist?"

Bettje hated to admit she didn't know. "We'll ask Father." She waited to catch her breath.

Two men strolled by scanning the doorways. Bettje heard one say, "Oh, you'll recognize him without any trouble. He's stout and gets red in the face easily."

"Are you sure he lives on this street?"

"Quite sure. He's been followed for some time, in secret of course. We even know where he goes at night—Jan Claes' house. One of these days we'll pounce, but not now. Wait until he's preaching his pernicious message to a big group of his misguided followers and then we'll turn all of them over to the church for cross-examination."

The underlying threat sent a chill of terror down Bettje's spine. What had Father done? What kind of work did he do at night? Why did people spy on him? She would have to warn him at once. She ran ahead of Jan straight to Father's study.

14

Father sat at a thick oak table, his Bible with its corded back open on one side of him, and his writing paper and ink in front. As usual, he had put his pen behind his ear.

"Where's my pen?" Father greeted her. "Did either of you children take it?"

Bettje could not smile this time at the familiar joke. "It's on your ear, Father." She sat on a bench in front of him and tried to think what she was going to say. This time Father must not brush her off with his "When you are older, I'll explain."

Someone knocked at the back door. Lukas Lambert stumbled in. "The authorities—they've got him—my nephew." His voice quivered. "Caught him this morning trying to escape by boat. Menno, you know what this means."

Father flushed and closed his eyes for a moment.

"But I didn't come here just to tell you that," the old man went on, "though my nephew is all the family I have. Menno, you are our leader. You must not allow yourself to be taken. The authorities know all about you. They are waiting to trap you some night soon when you're with the brethren. Leave Amsterdam. Leave tonight." Lukas' voice steadied and deepened in his urgent appeal.

Father put his arm around the old man's shoulder. "Why should they hate me when out of pure zeal I teach and explain in its purity the doctrine of Christ and His apostles? Let them deal with me as they like." He straightened. "Let them persecute and kill as they please. His Word will triumph."

Nothing Lukas said could change Father's determination to stay in Amsterdam as long as God willed.

When Lukas left, Bettje burst out, "Father, are

15

you an Anabaptist?"

In his surprise, Father knocked over his stool. "Never use that word again, Bettje." Then he whirled and asked, "Where did you hear it?"

Both Bettje and Jan told their story. Father paced the floor, then called to Mother, "Geertruydt, the dogs will soon be barking at our door."

"What does that mean, Father?" Jan asked.

"When you children are older, I'll explain." Father went to Mother's sickbed and took her hands in his. "No Scripture directs us to stay where we know beforehand that we will die or be in prison for life. We are admonished in plain words to flee from persecutors." He paused. "We shall have to leave Amsterdam."

Mother paled. "When?" she asked bravely.

"Tonight." He turned to Bettje and Jan. "You children each make a bundle of your clothes. You may take anything you can carry. The rest we shall have to leave behind."

In utter disbelief, Bettje fought back tears while she packed. The forbidden word *Anabaptist* rang through her mind. If only she had never heard it! In just one day, what misery this word had brought!

2 SURPRISE SUMMONS

A FEW weeks later on a quiet street in Emden, Bettje hurried Jan through the afternoon chill toward home.

"Don't go so fast, Bettje." Jan's frosty breath spiraled above his head. "I can't keep up."

Bettje blew on her numbed hands. "Serves you right. Mother worried all afternoon. You knew very well she couldn't come after you when she's sick, and I was busy with the baby."

"Does Father know I was gone?"

"No. He's been writing all afternoon. How many times has he told both of us to stay close to the house?" Bettje went on in a burst of indignation.

"But I heard him tell Mother Emden is the safest place there is because of Countess Anna," Jan argued.

"I heard that, too. Just the same we aren't to go running around talking to people."

"But I didn't talk to anyone."

"Then why did you go so far away?"

"I get tired of staying home all the time. I want to see what other people are doing," Jan explained.

"You won't tell Father on me, will you?"

"I ought to," Bettje said. "You know what he says about children obeying their parents."

"But I didn't do anything wrong. All I did was watch people go in and out of their houses. I didn't say a word. Please, Bettje, don't tell."

Bettje relented. "All right, I won't, but you'll have to help with supper, and you can feed the baby. Besides, I couldn't interrupt Father now, anyway—not when he's writing. You know what that means."

Jan stopped. "Another trip?" he groaned. "Why can't he stay home?"

Bettje laughed. "Why should he when *you* don't? Anyhow, he has to earn a living like all fathers."

"But he doesn't bring any money back when he goes on these trips," Jan said. "He only earns money when he digs peat, or mends dikes, or milks cows."

At the mention of cows, Bettje sighed. When the family had moved from Amsterdam to Emden, she had hoped for a cow of their very own, but Father said it was impossible to keep a cow in town.

Heavy footsteps crunched behind them.

Jan jerked Bettje's arm. "Someone's following us."

Bettje's pulses throbbed with sudden fear. What if someone tried to talk to them?

"Run!" she commanded. Jan obeyed. Their shoes clattered over the cobbled street.

A man called out, "Wait!"

In a spurt of terror, Bettje ran faster, with Jan right behind. The man shouted again and started to run. In a moment he overtook them and blocked their way. Bettje forced herself to look up. A bearded young man with a fur-lined hood circling his head panted, "Don't get alarmed. I just want some informa-

18

tion." His cultivated voice soothed Bettje's fears somewhat. "Do you children live around here?"

Bettje and Jan ducked their heads and did not reply.

"Can't either of you say something?" the young man asked in puzzlement. "I have an important summons here for a man who lives in this neighborhood. His name is Menno Simons. Do you know him?"

At the sound of their father's name, Bettje squeezed Jan's hand in warning.

"Ah, I can see that the name is familiar. Just tell me if you know him, yes or no."

Bettje and Jan remained silent.

"Haven't you children been taught to tell the truth?" the young man asked.

The question confused Bettje. Of course they had been taught to tell the truth, but should she tell the truth or obey Father's command not to talk to people? She had often heard Father say truth would win. Not only that, but he had said by God's grace he possessed nothing but unyielding truth. What should she say now?

"We're not allowed to talk to anyone," she stammered.

The young man fumbled inside his cloak and brought out a rolled paper. "This is a very important invitation for Menno Simons. I know he is in hiding, but he must have this paper. I assure you I am not a traitor."

Jan looked up. "What's a traitor?"

"Someone who pretends to be a friend but isn't," the young man explained. "Now, I can tell by your faces that you children know something about Menno Simons. Just show me his house. You won't have to say a word."

Bettje hesitated. What if Father should have this important paper?

"You wouldn't be telling a lie," the young man urged.

Was there a difference between telling a lie and *living* one? Bettje tried to think about it. Then she remembered. Father had often said, "God hates all liars."

She rubbed her numb hands in silence. The young man sighed. "I think I understand. No one must learn where Menno Simons lives. I won't insist, even though it will make a lot of trouble for me."

Bettje and Jan waited for the man to walk out of sight and ran home. The rented house, tucked side by side between the other houses on the street, had never seemed so welcome. Inside, Father and Mother waited near the hearth fire with Mariken, the baby.

Bettje faced a new problem. How could she tell Father about the message unless Jan confessed he had run away?

Father looked up. Bettje knew he was waiting to hear them explain where they had been so long. But she had promised Jan she would not tell on him. Jan sat down on a bench before the fire, his head tucked between his hunched shoulders, the picture of guilt.

Father must have known what Jan had done, Bettje decided. With a serious expression, Father stood Jan in front of him. "If I do not set my children an example, if I do not direct them at all times to Christ and His word, if I do not seek their salvation with all my heart, then I will not escape my punishment."

A worried expression crossed Jan's face, but he

said nothing. Bettje could see how puzzled he was. How could Father be punished for the disobedience of his child?

Father went on. "If I see my neighbor's ox fallen in a pit, or under the weight of a burden, I do not leave until I have given help. How much more should I be concerned for my children lying beneath the burden of their sins?"

At the word *children*, Jan cast a worried glance toward Bettje. She knew he appreciated her not telling on him.

Father waited a moment, then spoke more sternly. "If I do not punish the disobedience of the young with a rod and the older with the tongue," he began.

Jan burst into tears. "But Bettje didn't do anything. She just came after me."

"Why did she have to come after you?"

"Because I ran away." Jan dug his fists into his streaming eyes.

Father chided Jan. "If people find out where we live, we may have to move again. You must obey your parents and tell the truth at all times. Now, store this away in the little box of your conscience."

"A man stopped us," Jan said. "He wanted to see you, but we didn't tell, did we, Bettje?"

"He had an invitation for you," Bettje explained.

Father listened to the story. "It's as clear as daylight," he told Mother. "Even Emden, it appears, is not going to be safe for us." He stirred the fire. "No one except the brethren should know I am here."

"Was that man a traitor?" Jan asked.

Father and Mother exchanged worried glances.

"Why should they spare me?" he asked Mother.

"But Countess Anna is tolerant of the new religions," Mother murmured.

Then a visitor came, one of the Emden brethren. Father invited him to sit with the family around the fire. At first the visitor talked to Father in a low voice.

"What!" Father burst out after a moment. "You told John a Lasco that I'm living here in Emden? Don't you realize there are traitors everywhere? Just today someone tried to force the children to tell where I live." Father's deep, resonant voice rose to an exasperated pitch. "The next thing you know, I will be called by many who have neither seen nor heard me a deceiving heretic."

Jan leaned toward Bettje. "What's a heretic?"

"I don't know." Jan's question bothered Bettje. Father used many strange words. In the last few weeks she had listened with care to every word Father said. She knew now that he preached to people and wrote books to help them understand the Word of God and obey it. He had said people were inwardly chock-full of unrighteousness. "The whole world walks unconcerned and without fear," she remembered him saying. "They all walk on the evil, crooked way and not on the way of the Lord."

Why had one of the brethren revealed Father's hiding place in Emden? Bettje listened to the visitor explain.

"Menno, you completely misunderstand the situation," the visitor said. "You must know that Countess Anna has appointed John a Lasco to organize religion here, and he has planned a meeting on January 28 for two or three days."

"I shall not go." Father's forceful voice carried above his visitor's. "Why would you press me to go before the public? Do you not know I could not do so without blood and death?"

"But, Menno, this meeting is not public—"

Father interrupted. "There are traitors everywhere." He stared at the hearth fire. "However, I would freely offer myself if you can show one plain passage in the Scriptures that the apostles and prophets have publicly spoken at such places where they knew that the people had decided to kill them, as, alas, they have everywhere done concerning the brethren."

The visitor tugged at his beard in annoyance. "Let me say again, Menno, the meeting is not public. In the first place, many Reformed preachers have found safety here in Emden. In the second place, John a Lasco guarantees your personal safety to and from this meeting. In the third place, he has more power than even the magistrates."

Bettje could see this remark angered Father.

"Where do we find more ungodliness than among those in authority?" he snapped. "Are we to openly wheedle and flatter the magistrates, so bluntly contrary to the Scriptures?" He seized the poker and stirred the fire until the sparks flew.

"Why, Menno, are you saying that John a Lasco wheedles and flatters? Remember, he is nobly born and does not need to stoop to such measures."

Father folded his arms. "I fear that your John a Lasco, like other preachers, is hired and bought for a salary and does not preach unless hired. The John a Lascos of the world do not teach because of Christian love and the Holy Spirit. They serve for money. Anyone who denies this will also deny that the sun shines during the day. People want to hear preachers who tickle their ears. They are more like clods than Christians. Truth would be hated even if spoken by Christ Himself from heaven."

"Be that as it may, you must admit, Menno, that these Reformed preachers, much as you sneer at them, preach from the Bible."

"I admit this—that the preachers of the world like to be greeted as lords and masters. John a Lasco, I know, is really proud of his noble birth, but did you ever read of Doctor Isaiah, or Master Ezekiel, or Lord Paul, or hear or read that the holy apostles and prophets loved to be called by such high vain names as do the learned ones and the preachers of the world? Let the Lord Jesus Christ and His apostles be your doctors and teachers in the matter and not the ambitious preachers of this world." Father added, "I will write about this at length."

The visitor stood up. "Menno, I think you are being stubborn about the proposed meeting in January."

Father laughed and invited him to eat with the family. Bettje and Jan helped Mother prepare an early supper.

"Father talks a lot, doesn't he?" Jan whispered. Mother warned him with a glance.

Everyone sat down to the table, and after grace Father and his visitor continued to talk.

"I might as well confess, Menno, that John a Lasco asked me if you preached only at night."

Father's eyes snapped. "I have taught far more in the daytime. If I were to go to this meeting I would remind him that the apostles also at times preached at night. Although my co-workers and I do not teach at public meetings where all men meet, the truth is not hushed up but is preached here and there both by day and by night, in cities and country, with tongue and pen, at the peril of life—but not in public meetings."

"John a Lasco also asked where your church is."

Father laughed. "You know as well as I. I would tell him my church is in houses, fields, forests, and wastes." He glanced at the visitor. "What else did he ask?"

The visitor cleared his throat. "He thought you would be much safer if you conformed somewhat more than you do."

With his spoon halfway to his mouth, Father retorted, "Christ does not say, 'Preach the doctrines and commands of men, nor preach councils and customs, nor preach the ideas and opinions of the learned.' He says, 'Preach the gospel.' It is not enough that in appearance a man speaks much of the Word of the Lord. A devout and unblamable conduct must also be seen, as the Scriptures teach."

"Perhaps," Mother ventured, "you should go to the meeting."

"If I did go," Father said with enthusiasm, "I would stop the mouth of all opponents with the power of a true doctrine. We must all be governed by the plainly expressed commands of Christ. The wisdom of God which my co-workers and I teach is a wisdom which none may understand except those who are desirous of living and walking according to the will of God. Whoever does not pray much and keep himself in the fear of the Lord cannot stand."

Bettje had never heard Father talk so much. Did he talk to people like this at night?

"Why not go to the meeting and explain all that?" Mother suggested.

"If I did go, I would speak for a church 'not having spot or wrinkle.' I would remind all these Reformed preachers, 'For other foundation can no man lay than that is laid, which is Jesus Christ.' "

The visitor rose to go. "May I tell John a Lasco that you will come to the conference January 28?"

Father looked at Mother, then nodded yes.

After the visitor left, Jan stood looking out the door. "Father, someone is watching our house from across the street."

"It must be one of the brethren," Father said.

Mother looked out. "No. I never saw him before. He's too well dressed for one of our brethren."

"This means I cannot go to the meeting tonight," Father said. "I see that even in Emden I cannot be assured of safety. Of course," he told Mother, "I have already prepared for this day, but I did not expect it to be so soon."

"Whatever must be done, we'll do," Mother said.

"But you haven't been well—"

"I'll manage—with God's help," Mother smiled.

Bettje knew what was going to happen. Jan, too, seemed to sense what was taking place. Bettje braced herself for Father's decision.

"We shall have to leave Emden," he announced.

With sudden understanding, Bettje realized their family would always be on the move. They would never be able to have a cow. She choked back the tears. If only they could live in one place like other people!

3   FAMILY SECRET

AT twilight the next day Father helped his family into a rowboat one of the brethren had loaned. Bettje sat on the back seat. The canal lay quiet, somehow watchful, even dangerous. Nearby trees overshadowed the water and moved in the cold wind.

Bettje strained to see. Was someone even now spying on them, or was it only the movement of the branches that she saw? Beside her, Jan hunched down, his peaked cap over his eyes, his chin muffled in his cloak. Mother sat on the seat ahead, Mariken in her arms. Father shoved the boat from the dock and rowed inland, away from Emden. Neighborhood dogs barked a frantic farewell to the family.

Father had said when dogs barked, captors might be near. But why would anyone want to capture Father?

Bettje leaned forward. "Where are we going?" she whispered to Mother. With a warning finger to her lips, Mother turned and shook her head. Bettje quivered with a nameless fear. Dim memories crowded her mind. Weren't there times even before they had moved from Amsterdam when Father hurried his family away? Why? Cold and miserable, Bettje fought down the protests that sprang to her lips. Why did Father's preaching make his family suffer?

The boat glided between narrow banks along flat meadowland, the grass dark green from recent rain. Sometimes the boat passed cows in the pastures. How beautiful they looked! Once Bettje glimpsed through the open door of a thatched-roof cottage a cheerful hearth fire with the family around it in a semicircle, dry and warm. An inner rebellion rose up and almost choked her.

"Why can't we live like other people?" she thought. If only Father would stay long enough in one place to buy a cow! Oh, to have a cow to milk every single day like other people in Friesland! The long-suppressed desire swelled up within Bettje until she could contain it no longer.

"Father, will you buy us a cow?" The minute the words were out, she could have bitten her tongue. Of all times to confide her secret wish! Why hadn't she kept still? Father was so tense and worried about the family's safety, he had no time to think of anything else.

"A *cow?*" Father burst into a sudden laugh and leaned on the oars for a moment. "A cow?" he repeated. "Oh, no. Dear me, no."

"Bettje," Mother chided, "how could you think of a cow at a time like this?"

Bettje huddled deep into her cloak. Her cheeks burned with embarrassment. Father loved to tease, and later, when they were safe, she knew he would never let her forget what she had said.

At her side Jan straightened up. "Why do we have to move again?" he blurted. "Why is everything a secret?"

"Hush," Mother said over her shoulder. "Your father has good reasons for what he does. When you children are old enough to understand, he will explain. Now, we don't want to hear another word from either of you. Children must always obey their parents without question."

Father grunted agreement. His face had reddened with the strain of rowing. Why did his preaching bring danger so often to their doorstep so that he had to whisk his family away instead of helping people? What was Father's secret? Who were the people who knew it?

The questions boiled through Bettje's head. How could she find out the answers if Father and Mother wouldn't explain?

The boat slid past slender trees bordering the canal. Bettje watched the night shadows deepen. One shadow moved unexpectedly. Bettje caught her breath. Someone on horseback was keeping pace with them on the other side of the canal. Or was it only a cow moving about? The mere possibility embarrassed Bettje afresh. She did not dare call Father's attention to the moving shadow. He might laugh at her.

In the distance a torch light flickered. Father pulled harder on the oars. "We're almost there," he panted. "I arranged with one of the brethren today to help us."

Mother shivered and held the baby closer. "I hope they have found us a safe place to stay."

Just before complete darkness set in, Father nosed the boat into a tiny inlet behind a house. A man with a lantern ran up. "You're here at last, safe and sound! Easy on the oars, though," he warned. "The mud is thick."

The warning came too late. Father had run the boat aground.

"Never mind," the man with the lantern said. "At least you're safe for the time being, Menno. Did anyone see you leave?"

"I thought for a moment the dogs would give us away," Father replied, "but no one saw us."

Bettje was torn with indecision. Should she mention the man on horseback? But what if she were mistaken? How could anyone know they were leaving? Father had sneaked them out the back way one by one and hidden them at the home of one of the brethren until time to leave. Besides, Father was with a friend now. There would surely be no danger.

"Menno, you're to have my house all to yourselves during your stay here," Father's friend said.

"But what about you and your wife?" Father asked.

"We're staying with my son on the next farm." The man pointed across the meadow. "But now let's unload the boat." He shouldered a bundle and started toward the house. Jan tried to jump from the boat to the dock. He slipped and sank knee-deep in mud. When the men pulled him out, both shoes had been sucked off.

"They're lost," Father's friend stated. "But now is not the time to worry about that. We must unload the boat quickly and hide it so that no curious neighbors will ask questions."

Afterward, when the family was alone in the house, Bettje helped Mother make beds. Mother sank into a broad-backed chair before the fire. With a pang

Bettje realized Mother was still far from well. Jan, too, seemed listless and tired. He warmed his bare feet before the fire. Bettje glimpsed his wan, thin face and knew he was going to be sick. Two sick people on her hands! Mariken, the baby, would be the least trouble of all to take care of. Still, with a comfortable house to live in and a cheerful fire, Bettje did not mind the extra work that faced her. Nevertheless, she had not forgotten, not for a minute, that she was going to find out the family secret. When she found two empty cow stalls by the kitchen she remembered her secret dream with a sigh.

The next day Mother doled out a few coins from the long purse at her waist. "You must take Jan to the shoemaker in the village and buy him a pair of shoes," she told Bettje. "Stay there until the shoes are ready, but don't say anything more than you have to."

Bettje and Jan walked down a cow path to the new village. It was not hard to find the shoemaker's shop in the front room of a little house facing the main road. The shoemaker, a bright-eyed, small man with gray hair, greeted them with a lift of his grizzled eyebrows. "I don't believe I know you two. Newcomers, be'n't you?"

Bettje and Jan exchanged glances. Bettje felt an alarm bell ring within her. How should they answer? Should they answer at all?

"You don't have to tell me," the shoemaker said after a moment. "In these times, it is better not to talk." He did not even ask how Jan had lost his shoes. "I think I have a pair that will fit you, but I'll have to hollow the insides a little more."

"Then we'll wait." Bettje pulled Jan to a bench in the corner.

An officer of the town approached the shop. The shoemaker did not lose a beat of his tiny shoe hammer. "Better turn your backs," he advised. "You might sort out that pile of leather scraps in the corner, big ones in one pile, little ones in another."

Bettje hardly breathed. Had they been discovered already? Would the officer track down Father?

"How are things going?" the officer asked.

"Fine." The shoemaker's voice tightened.

"Lots of shoes to make and mend?"

"Yes." The tap of the hammer quickened.

"The parson says you haven't been coming to church lately."

"I have shoes to deliver. I go to church elsewhere."

"Do you swear to this?"

"Swearing is forbidden to Christians."

"You sound like an Anabaptist. Are you sure you are not one of them?"

"Do I look like an Anabaptist?" The shoemaker forced a laugh.

The officer cleared his throat. "If any unusual orders come in, report them to me. We are trying to trap an upriser."

In spite of herself, Bettje's hand jerked. The pile of scraps she had built up toppled over. Jan helped her arrange it again. Bettje knew without a word being spoken that the shoemaker would not report Jan's new shoes.

The officer went out. A little later Bettje heard two horses neigh outside. She looked up. Two horsemen dismounted in front of the shop. One looked like a nobleman because of his fine-textured coat lined with fur. He held a broken strap in one hand. A younger man stepped toward the shop with the nobleman. Bettje gasped in horror. She had recognized the man who had stopped Jan and her in Emden. She made Jan crouch with her behind the bench and watch.

"My good man," the nobleman said to the shoemaker, "could you do me a favor and bolt this strap together? There seems to be no other place in this little hamlet where I can get it fixed, and we have much traveling to do. I will pay well."

The shoemaker took the strap and began to mend it.

"I don't see how you lost track of him," the older man told the younger. "This will hardly endear you to Countess Anna, or me either. I shouldn't have to be running over the countryside like this. That was your job. In the first place, why did he flee? Something must have awakened his suspicions."

The young man shrugged. "I don't know about that. One of the so-called brethren pointed him out. I followed him here today when he came alone, and then I followed him when he brought his family. It grew so dark I lost track of them. They and their boat just disappeared."

Bettje clenched her fists. She should have told Father about the rider on horseback.

"He's the scourge and plague of the country," the nobleman said. "He appears by night, stealthily preaching his blasphemous second baptism—I'm quoting Gellius Faber, of course. You should see Gellius' face when he talks about it." The nobleman laughed. "You've heard of Gellius, haven't you?"

"The ex-priest from Jelsum?"

The nobleman nodded. "He joined the Reformed Church and became a minister at Norden and then at Emden in 1538." The nobleman chuckled. "He goes by two other names when it suits him—Jelle Smit and Faber de Bouma. I don't know what name he'll assume at the January conference, but I know I'll have a hard time keeping him quiet." He hummed a little, then asked, "What did you think of the edict of '42?"

"You forget, sir, that I have been in Germany at the university. I haven't kept up with all the decrees against the Anabaptists. What was this one—any different from the first one in 1525?"

"Just more desperate. Our man is slippery as an eel—as evidenced by how he slipped from under your fingers."

The younger man winced. "He's around here someplace."

"Then you'd better find him. Countess Anna could do you many favors and put you into court life if you do what she asks of you."

"Ah, how open you are about your worldly ambitions! Is this the usual way of men of the Reformed Church?" the young man asked with a sly grin.

The nobleman shrugged. "A man must live. As it happens, if I hadn't just by accident run across some of our friend's followers in Emden, I wouldn't have known where to turn. They all swore that he lived in town, but as you well know, by the time I arrived the house was empty. The bird had flown." The nobleman pulled out a paper from inside his coat. "Here's a map of the countryside where more brethren lie in hiding. There are more curlicues, curves, canals, and cow paths than you can imagine. Every X stands for an Anabaptist in hiding. Our friend is certainly covering the country. I understand he shoos his wife and three children ahead of him or behind, as the case may be."

"How long have the authorities been after him?"

"It all started in January 1536. You heard about that, I suppose. By October of that year—the twenty-fourth, if I recall correctly, two brothers, Herman and Gerrit Jansz, were sentenced to death in Leeuwarden because they had lodged him near Witmarsum. Still, if he had not paid them that secret visit in October, they probably would not have been sentenced. But what can you expect of a preacher who insists on preaching in meadows, shops, attics—and at night? He's quite a night traveler, as you know."

The nobleman laughed softly.

The young man winced. "What was the edict you mentioned?"

"Let me put it this way. If you have any crime on your books, you'll not only be forgiven, but Leeuwarden offers you one hundred guilders for turning Menno Simons over to the executioner."

The shoemaker's hammer clattered to the floor. With a murmur of apology he picked it up.

Bettje's eyes widened with shock. She now understood everything! So this was the family secret Father did not want them to know!

4   THE MEETING PLACE

FATHER must be warned at once.

"Do they want to *kill* Father?" Jan whispered.

"Not those men—the authorities."

"We've got to tell him." Jan started up from behind the bench.

Bettje pulled him down. "Not now. Don't let them see you." If only they would leave!

"Have you seen or heard of this man?" the nobleman asked the shoemaker.

"What did you say his name is?" the shoemaker asked with an expressionless face.

"Menno Simons."

"What does he look like?"

"Well, from the notices I have read on church doors and town halls over the countryside, he's plump, with wide-spaced eyes and curly beard."

"Does he wear fine clothes like you?"

The nobleman flushed. "Menno wears very plain clothes—a wide-brimmed hat, with round crown, and triangular, cheek-hugging flaps, a style I never cared for. I understand he sometimes wears a round black cap, reminiscent of his former profession. His neck is circled with a ruff, like most people's, and his coat is held by pegs, like lots of people, though what he has against buttons, I don't know. They have been used since the eleventh century."

"I haven't seen anyone of that description," the shoemaker said with such finality that the nobleman and the young man stared. "Here is your strap." He waved aside the nobleman's money. "No, this costs you nothing. Mending straps is not my regular work."

"Why, thank you. Thank you." The nobleman looked astonished and for the first time, ill at ease. He left with the young man.

The shoemaker helped Jan into his new shoes. "Too bad this Menno Simons can't be warned, if he's around here. I'm sure he wouldn't stay long with danger this close."

Bettje batted back tears. She would never complain about moving again—not if it meant Father's safety. She paid for Jan's shoes, and she and her brother hurried to their new home. Father was not there, and Mother had a visitor. Bettje played with Mariken and hoped the visitor, a talkative neighbor woman, would go away.

"I saw you move in last night," the woman confided, "and I said to myself, 'Why would any sensible people try to move into a place at night? Why didn't they wait until morning?'" She paused as if waiting for a reply, but Mother just smiled.

"Of course, if my cow hadn't been sick last night, I wouldn't have seen you folks at all. Still, now that I think of it, I remember seeing Schrevel taking his cows to his son's. That should have told me something strange was happening. Schrevel hadn't told anybody that he was selling the place."

Again the neighbor woman waited, but Mother did not volunteer any information. After a few more questions, which Mother avoided answering, the neighbor left.

Bettje poured out the morning incident in a burst of words. "We have to warn him, Mother," Bettje finished.

Mother put a hand to her forehead. "Is it starting again so soon?"

"Why do they want to kill Father?" Bettje asked. This time, Mother would surely explain.

"Someday you'll understand, but now you and Jan are too young."

"But, Mother—"

"We are not going to discuss this anymore. Now, about your father, there's no way to warn him yet. I don't know where he went. We'll just have to wait until he comes home."

The next day Bettje learned that Father had come home and left again after hearing Mother's warning. He would not stop his work with people, telling them about the Bible, and he would not move the family again until the last possible moment.

During the day, Bettje coaxed Jan into helping her smooth the sand in the cow stalls. "We might have a cow sometime." She traced a pattern on the sand. "I've been thinking about Father, and I've made up my mind. I'm going to find out exactly what Father does at night."

"But he'll tell us when we're old enough."

"Well, I'm old enough now, and so are you, even if you are a year younger than I am. I know the authorities want to capture Father. I know he explains the Bible and helps people find out about

God. But why is that bad? Why can't we live like other people in Friesland?"

"We do in some ways," Jan said. "Lots of times Father thatches roofs and digs peat and mends dikes. Other people do that."

"Yes, but they don't sit in their houses and write for hours. They don't have visitors who sneak in and out at dawn and dusk, and they don't go out at night and stay away for hours at a time."

Jan sifted a handful of sand through his fingers. "Unless they go to hear Father preach."

"This morning I saw a girl take two cows to pasture." Bettje felt the old longing rise unexpectedly in her. "She does it every day, I know." She swirled the sand into a design. "We've got cow stalls. We ought to have a cow."

"But we're in a borrowed house, and if we have to move again, we couldn't take a cow with us in a rowboat on the canal." Jan grinned at Bettje, and in spite of herself, she giggled at the picture. "What does Father do at night in his preaching that the authorities don't like?" Jan went on.

"I don't know," Bettje admitted.

"Father is always talking about traitors around." Jan seemed proud that he knew what the word meant.

"That's just it," Bettje exclaimed. "Oh, Jan, I almost forgot. Yesterday I heard Father tell Mother the most exciting story about a traitor. This man was coming with an officer in a boat to arrest Father, and they met Father in a boat going the opposite way. Well, Father just knew something was wrong, and as soon as he passed them, he jumped ashore. Then he heard the traitor call out, 'Behold, the bird has escaped.' The officer raged and ranted. 'Why didn't you call out sooner so we could have caught him?' Then the traitor said, 'I could not speak. My tongue was bound.' "

"When did that happen?" Jan was astonished.

"Some time ago, but he never told Mother about it for fear she'd worry."

"Why did he tell her yesterday?"

"Because he just found out this traitor was executed for not turning Father over to the officers."

Jan was silent for a moment. "Why does Father keep on preaching when he knows he might be put to death, too?"

"That's what I want to know, and I'm going to find out."

Jan sat down at the edge of a stall. "How?"

"It's a secret." At Jan's hurt look, Bettje relented. "I'll tell you when it happens."

"That's not fair."

Bettje reconsidered. She had to tell someone about her daring plan. "Some nights Father goes out and talks to people."

"Are you going to try to stop him?"

"Of course not."

"Then what do you mean?" Jan's brows furrowed with thought. "Oh, Bettje, are you going to *follow* him?"

"Yes, the next chance I get. I've made up my mind."

"I'm going, too," Jan announced.

"Promise you won't tell Mother or Father beforehand?"

"I promise."

Secretly delighted, Bettje watched for the right

time. One night after supper, Father sat before the hearth fire in a cane-backed chair, opened his big Bible, and read aloud. Bettje and Jan sat at his feet and listened. Even with Mother not well, Bettje felt the warmth and security she loved to feel. If only every night could be like this! Soon Mother fell asleep. Someone tapped at the door.

Father closed the Bible. "See who it is," he told Bettje.

It was the owner of the house. He beckoned to someone behind him. "Here is a man who is troubled about the church," he told Father. "I told him you would help. I didn't mention your name," he whispered. "Let him be won over first." The owner left.

The newcomer, a small man with full beard, blinked at the bright firelight, ducked his head, and shuffled his feet. At Father's invitation, he sat before the fire.

"What troubles you?" Father asked.

"The church. I cannot believe the priests any longer," the man burst out, "but where can I turn?"

"Believe God's holy Word." Father's firm voice rang out. "Only follow the Word of God and the matter is settled. We are to be governed by the plain commands of Christ and the pure doctrines and practice of His holy apostles."

"I don't know," the man faltered. "The priests say—"

"If men will not believe the Word of God, neither I nor any other man can help them."

The voices woke Mother. "Menno," she called.

The visitor's face paled. His lips formed the word *Menno*. "There's only one Menno," he murmured

42

with a fear-stricken glance at Father. "I didn't realize—"

"Didn't realize what?" Father asked.

"Are you the Menno—Simon's son—who has deceived many and led them down the road to their destruction, as I have heard? Are you that murderer of souls and bodies, too, so that to be seen with you brings death?" The little man stood up and eyed the door.

Father was matter-of-fact. "I am loaded down behind my back with slanders and lies by those who wish me ill. People are always trying to saddle me with things of which I am not guilty." He added as an afterthought, "I guess I was born to turn my ear to the slanderer and my back to the scourger. They have not despised me but the Word of God."

The little man stared at Father with horror. "But you are one of those terrible Munsterites," he said, as if Father had not said a word.

Father sighed. "Those who persecute us say that we are like those of Munster, but the Munsterites acted contrary to the Word of God in many things. We deny that we are one with them. We have never eaten, drunk, or had any communion with them unless they renounced their errors. We are basically different from the Munsterites. We honor earthly power and kings."

The little man looked partly convinced. "On what do you base your beliefs?"

" 'For other foundation can no man lay than that is laid, which is Jesus Christ,' " Father said with flashing eyes. "He is our Master and Teacher, our Redeemer, Savior, and eternal Mediator."

"But doesn't the church say this, too?"

Father shook his head. "You must hear the holy Word and harvest the fruits of righteousness, such as the fear and love of God, mercy, temperance, humility, truth, and the joy in the Holy Ghost. But the gospel knows not such strange fruits as infant baptism, masses, matins, vespers, caps, crucifixes, chapels, altars, and bells. God has not commanded them, either through Christ His Son, or through the apostles and prophets."

The visitor tugged at his beard. "If the doctrine you preach is true, why doesn't everybody know about it?"

"The number of true believers is, sad to say, very small. The number of the unrighteous is very great. Christ Jesus and His eternal truth must ever dwell with the few in retired places. Read the Bible yourself. You will find that the number of the elect was always small."

Bettje could see that the visitor was becoming more and more convinced that Father was right. Nevertheless, the little man continued his questions.

"Why do you teach secretly at night?"

Father sighed. "Is it not more praiseworthy to teach the pure saving truth at night when we cannot meet openly in the daytime than in the daytime to shout deceiving lies from a pulpit as has, alas, been openly done these many years before the whole world?"

"Then you are not keeping this truth a secret?"

"The true church," Father said, "can as little be hid as a city upon a hill or a candle upon a candlestick. I tell the truth and lie not. I am no Enoch. I am no Elias. I am no seer, nor prophet who can teach other than what is written in the Word of God and understood in the Spirit."

The visitor seemed fascinated by Father's sincerity. Bettje saw Father frown. Was he worried about the reference to his night preaching?

"The truth," Father told his visitor, "is not kept by us as a secret but is preached here and there, both by day and at night, in cities and country places, by mouth and through the printed page, by living example and by martyrdom."

At the word *martyrdom*, the visitor shuddered. "Are you against all law?"

"Oh, dear, no! I willingly obey all human ordinances, if they be not against God."

"What about your twice baptizing?" the visitor asked. "After all, are you not called Re-Baptizers and Anabaptists?"

"If we are Anabaptists because we repeat a baptism instituted by man, then was Paul an Anabaptist for rebaptizing those who were of understanding minds?"

"The church does not agree with you."

"The church needs the eye salve which is mentioned in the Revelation of John," Father retorted.

"People think you possess some strange power."

"By God's grace I possess nothing but powerful truth," Father said. "I have no visions or angelic inspirations. Nor do I desire them, lest I be deceived. The Word of Christ alone is sufficient. I say again, believe God's holy and infallible Word and seek true repentance, which I have taught all along."

"Where can I hear more of your message?" the visitor asked.

Bettje heard Father say something in a tone too

low for her to make out the words. He and the visitor went out together.

"Tonight is the night," Bettje whispered to Jan in growing excitement. When she was sure Mother and the baby were sleeping soundly, she and Jan bundled up in warm clothes and went outside into the cold night, thankful that there was enough moonlight for them to make out the path. But which direction should they go? Perhaps across the meadow to the place where the owner of their borrowed house was staying. She and Jan started across. In the dim light Bettje made out the shadowy forms of fifteen or twenty people huddled close. She and Jan crept closer, shying from every rustle, alert to every sound. They stayed well behind the group, near a clump of bushes. Father was talking to the group encircling him.

Bettje heard a movement behind her. Terror-stricken, she grabbed Jan's arm. A man holding a dark lantern edged past them. Was he one of Father's people? Bettje couldn't see the man's face. He stood behind the others and listened. Bettje decided she had been too suspicious. Father was preaching.

"Now is the time to awake from the sleep of our ugly sins. Now is the day of salvation," Father told his listeners. "It will not help a fig to be called Christians so long as we are not converted from this wicked, immoral, and shameful life of the flesh. Seek your new birth and the new life which must be kept unblamable before God and all the world. Be of good cheer and doubt not, for the Lord will strengthen your souls. Truth will remain truth forever."

His listeners murmured assent and turned to each other in mutual agreement, but the man with the lantern did not talk to the others. A woman suddenly

exclaimed, "There is someone here who doesn't belong. It's an officer!"

At once the others exclaimed, "We'll be arrested! Run! Hide!"

The group scattered in all directions. To Bettje's horror, she saw the man with the lantern grasp Father's arm. The dark lantern the man held illuminated both their faces. Bettje stifled a gasp. It was the young man who had stopped them in Emden, the man who had followed them on horseback, the man who had been with the nobleman at the shoemaker's. He had trapped Father!

5 MESSAGE FROM AMSTERDAM

THE young man thrust a rolled paper into Father's hands. "You must be Menno Simons. I've been trying to find you for days. I am an assistant to John a Lasco. You have heard of this nobleman, no doubt. Countess Anna appointed him to organize the new religions here in Friesland. He came himself today to invite you to a discussion on January 28, but you are a difficult man to find, and he had to go back to Emden without seeing you himself."

"Why does John a Lasco summon that old heretic Menno, who appears to be as slippery as an eel caught by the tail?"

Taken aback by Father's joking manner, the young man smiled uncertainly. "It is to be a friendly discussion."

Father uttered a short laugh. "A friendly discussion about religion? Dear me. Am I to approve of the dark smoke of an ear-pleasing preacher like John a Lasco? But I suppose he has to trump up something."

"John a Lasco offers you an invitation to defend your sect," the young man said with dignity.

"What smooth talk he uses," Father said. "It is a small matter to be called sect-makers by the world. The children of God from apostolic times were called that. But go on."

Father beamed at the young man. Bettje could see he enjoyed talking.

"John a Lasco hopes for unity among the Reformed preachers."

"His hope is like thistledown before the wind," Father retorted.

"But you will have a chance to talk to several learned ones," the young man began.

Father smiled. "The sly way of the learned ones is great, but I have preferred to be the fool of the world's learned ones in order that I might be found of God to be wise, rather than to be one of the most famous of the worldly wise and at the last be a fool in God's sight. I would tell them so and trust that this bold and blunt language would be understood. In short, I have become quite tired of the leaven and the swine husks of the learned ones. I see no reason whatever for attending this discussion."

"But Hermann Brassius will be there, and Gellius Faber," the young man said in desperation.

"Gellius Faber!" Father echoed. "He who calls me Anabaptist, night preacher, and other derogatory names? I shall most certainly be at this meeting. Where and when does it take place?"

"At the chapel of the old Franciscan monastery in Emden, on January 28. No doubt you are familiar with monasteries?" The young man's voice held an edge of mockery. He continued in a politer tone, "Then I may assure John a Lasco that you will be in Emden on the appointed day?"

"I am willing and prepared at all times, as long as I have breath or sense and can sit on a wagon or lie in a ship to appear before Gellius or anybody to defend the foundation of our faith, just so it takes place *under safe conduct,* in good faith," Father said.

"You will be given a *Safe Conduct.* Your safety is assured both to and from the meeting."

"Are any particular topics to be discussed?" Father asked.

"How Christ became human, infant baptism, original sin, sanctification, and the calling of preachers."

Father hummed with satisfaction. "I am willing to attend," he said. "If this is to be a free discussion with the preachers, either privately before witnesses or publicly before a full assembly, and if I cannot prove that the preachers one and all are deceivers and not pastors, then I will publicly acknowledge before all the world that we have forsaken the church of Christ."

On this crisp note the two men parted. Bettje and Jan hurried home and told no one of their visit to Father's meeting place. In the days that followed, Bettje heard Father discuss with Mother all that he intended to say at the conference.

One day the shoemaker came to the house. "I have been coming to your meetings," he told Father, "and I have heard about this conference in Emden. In my shop I hear many things." He paused, as if wondering how much to say. "There are some in Emden who are not friendly toward you. Our ruler, Countess Anna, is tolerant, but her brother the duke is not, especially toward Anabaptists. He has spies everywhere."

Father thanked the shoemaker for the warning and assured him of continual watchfulness. Assured of a *Safe Conduct* to and from the conference, Father arranged to stay with friends in Emden for a few days. The morning he left, Bettje and Jan walked almost all the way with him. Coming back they met the shoemaker leading a cow.

"Here—you children take this cow," he exclaimed with a worried glance over his shoulder. "I didn't know what to do with her, but God is with me. I'd rather see her in your hands than anybody I know."

Bewildered, Bettje took the leading rope. "But why are you giving her away?"

Instead of answering, the shoemaker asked, "Where is your father?"

"At the conference."

"You must go after him and warn him to leave here at once. Some woman reported to the authorities that I attended his meetings, and now my property is being confiscated. I hoped to sell my cow and leave East Friesland, but this way is better. You keep the cow and warn your father that he may be next."

With mixed feelings Bettje led the cow away. She and Jan had not gone far when they heard shouts. Looking back they saw two officials had closed in on the shoemaker, one on each side. Once again the loathsome word *Anabaptist,* shouted in hatred, came to their ears. The two officials fastened the shoemaker's arms behind his back and led him away.

"Will they do that to Father?" Jan asked in horror.

"He's been promised a *Safe Conduct*," Bettje said with an assurance she did not feel. Should they take the cow home, or should they tell Father what had happened?

"We've got to tell Father," Jan pleaded. "Can't we take the cow with us?"

Bettje agreed. In Emden they asked directions and came to the former monastery.

"We're looking for Father," Bettje explained to the guard at the big door.

"What's his name?" the guard asked.

But Bettje knew better than to call Father by name. "It's just Father. He'll know."

The guard scratched his capped head, then laughed. "It's about time for the session to be over. I'll announce you."

When the men streamed out, the guard cupped his hands. "There are two children here with a cow. They ask for Father. Who in here answers to the name of Father?"

A ripple of amusement spread among the men. Bettje saw Father in heated conversation with several men. He did not even turn around. One of the men Father talked to was the well-dressed nobleman Bettje had seen in the shoemaker's shop. A man with the nobleman scowled at Father.

"Gellius, you err no less than I should err if I refused to feed my children that cannot work because Paul said, 'He that does not labor shall not eat,' which is undeniably spoken in regard to those of mature years and not of children," Bettje heard Father say.

"Your doctrine deceives the simple," Gellius sneered.

"There is not a tiny tittle in the New Testament that children should be baptized," Father retorted.

"This from a false prophet?" Gellius asked.

"True faith is not found in children of two, three, or four years. Both the Scriptures and common sense teach us that." Father turned to the nobleman. "Does the noble and learned John a Lasco grant that the Scripture which mentions the matter speaks of adults?"

"I agree," John a Lasco said, "but Menno, you need not magnify my name like that."

"I do so only out of common politeness," Father said, and went on. "Does a ceremony which is practiced without the command of God have any promise?"

His listeners shook their heads.

"Is not such a ceremony which is practiced without the command of God idolatry?"

The others had to agree that Menno was right.

"Very well, worthy sirs, what then becomes of your infant baptism?"

Several men started to answer, but Gellius Faber's voice could be heard above the others. "Menno, if you insist upon a command, then show us where it is commanded that we should baptize believers."

" 'He that believeth and is baptized shall be saved,' " Father said. "Mark 16:16."

"That is not a command," the others protested, and cited how some translations of the twenty-eighth chapter of Matthew used the word *baptizing*.

"You are taking refuge behind a participle," Father exploded. "Luther has expressed it as a command. If I tell a servant to go and plow the ground, sowing it with wheat, although I use the principle

54

sowing, have I not commanded him to sow it with wheat?"

"Dear Menno, this is philosophy, not Scripture," John a Lasco said with a smile.

"I know very well that my truth will probably be held to be untrue in the eyes of the learned ones."

"Are you accusing us of lying?" Gellius flared. "There is but one church and one faith in the Old and New Testament. This conference," he told John a Lasco, "is a mistake."

Father held up his hand. "I beg you not to take it ill of me if when necessary I call a lie, a lie. By God's grace, I hope to do it without bitterness. I only want to clear myself with the truth, and since I find that so many in perversity of heart reject God's truth and delight in falsehood, I will be silent and speak not another word, for alas, it is all in vain."

Bettje could see that Father delighted to air his views.

"Who's a father here?" the guard called.

This time Father looked around. His mouth opened in amazement. "What are you doing here?" he asked Bettje and Jan. "Where did you get the cow?"

Bettje remembered the shoemaker and burst into tears. "You might be next," she sobbed. Father took the children aside and listened to the story. He agreed to let the family keep the cow and promised to teach the children how to milk.

Cheered by Father's promise, Bettje confided, "I'm going to call the cow *Mary.*"

An odd expression crossed Father's face, but he said nothing.

A few days later Bettje woke up at dawn with a start of fright. Someone was trying to get into the house. She could hear the intruder fumble at the door latch. She sprang out of bed and listened. The ominous swish and thump terrified her. She tried to call "Father," but the word stuck in her throat. Then she remembered. Father was still in Emden, although he had come home for a night after the conference. "Jan," she whispered. No answer. Jan lay in bed, curled up, one hand flung over his head, as if warding off a blow. Was someone coming after the family? Would they be taken away, like the shoemaker? It was no use trying to wake Jan. Bettje tiptoed past the hearth without stopping to warm her feet near the banked coals. At the kitchen door, Bettje put her ear to the keyhole. The swish and thump were distinct now, but somehow not frightening. Then she remembered the new cow, Mary, in her stall, and almost laughed aloud in relief.

Today she could milk the cow all by herself. Father had taught her. She opened the door. The cow rustled a welcome. Already she had destroyed the lovely sand patterns Bettje and Jan had made, but Bettje didn't mind. If only she didn't have to remember how the shoemaker had been taken away for being an Anabaptist! As she milked, Bettje reflected on what Father had told someone once. True faith, he had said, meant first disquiet, then peace; sorrow, then joy, but love of God made people joyful no matter what happened. Bettje sighed. How could such a belief be true? How could God allow such a kindly man as the shoemaker to be punished just because he had listened to Father?

That evening it was Jan's turn to bring the cow

in from pasture. He came back alone, white-faced.

"What happened? Where's Mary?"

"Wrapped around a willow tree near the canal. The rope got all twisted up."

"Well, unwind the rope and bring her home."

"I can't. There is a man out by the willow trees. He's watching the house." Jan wiped his face with his long-sleeved shirt. "I'm scared."

"But the cow has to be milked. She can't stay out there all night. We'll go out together." Bettje led the way outside.

A young man with a short beard came toward them at once. "I'm from Amsterdam." He tugged at his beard with nervous fingers. "You must be Bettje and Jan. I'm a friend of the nephew of an old man your father knew. I have a message for your father. Where is he?"

Since the messenger knew their names, Bettje was reassured. "He's in Emden."

"When will he be back?"

"Perhaps tonight."

"I can't stay. I must get back, but—"

"We could give Father the message," Bettje said.

"Oh, no," the messenger exclaimed in horror. "I couldn't tell children, and I know your mother hasn't been well. She shouldn't be burdened."

"Do you want to write it?" Bettje asked.

At first the messenger agreed. "But maybe you children can read. I know your father believes in teaching children how."

"Yes, I can read. Jan is just beginning. But we won't read your message if you don't want us to."

The messenger frowned. "I dare not write this. I'll wait out here for your father."

In a little while Father came in with the messenger.

"You remember Jan Claes, of course." The messenger seemed to have forgotten the whole family could hear him.

"What about him?" Father's voice sharpened with worry.

"He and Lukas Lambert, the old man, were martyred January 19," the messenger said in an unsteady voice.

"What does *martyred* mean?" Jan asked.

"Hush, Jan," Mother said. "When you are old enough, Father will explain." Her lips trembled and she put a hand over her mouth.

"It was because of your books, of course," the messenger went on. "I found out from a friend of mine, the nephew of old Lukas. My friend was caught, too, but he had no books of yours on him. He's still in prison, but he asked me to warn you."

Father clasped his hands. "If they burn my body, there is nothing more they can do. I've said it many times: Let them persecute and kill as they please. God's Word will triumph."

Bettje wept for kind, talkative old Lukas. Why did God let His people be killed? How long would Father stay alive?

6 THE "MISCHIEF MAKERS"

THE next day, after the messenger from Amsterdam left, Father sat by the fire and stared at the flames. Bettje and Jan hovered close.

"Father, I know what a martyr is," Jan burst out. "Lukas Lambert and Jan Claes were killed because they believed in God the way you do."

Father put his arms around Bettje and Jan. "I had hoped to spare you children such knowledge for a little while longer."

"Can't we move someplace where you'll always be safe?" Bettje asked.

Father hugged the children. "It doesn't matter where the place is, not a hair can fall from my head unless our heavenly Father sees it is best. So long as the appointed day and hour have not come, I am completely safe. Trust God with your whole hearts."

Bettje sighed with relief. In sudden understanding, she sensed that God's will was stronger than all the people in the world. She hoped the feeling would never leave her.

In the weeks that followed the Emden conference, Bettje and Jan studied harder than ever on their reading and writing lessons. If they knew the Scripture well, perhaps they could help Father someday. Father himself spent many hours writing the statement of faith he had promised John a Lasco.

One of the Reformed preachers who had been at the conference visited Father. Mother called Bettje and Jan to help her make cheese. The men's talk carried through the house clear to the empty stall where Mother had set the churn.

"Gellius Faber is one of the most learned men in Emden," Bettje heard the preacher say. "Don't you agree, Menno?"

"There are many unsuspecting hearts who look very much more to the learned ones than they do to Christ and His apostles," Father replied in a dry tone.

"But Gellius has won many hearts to God."

"To promise mountains of gold while not having sand hills to give is usually called boasting," Father returned.

The preacher cleared his throat. "I came here to tell you that some say you are working with the devil."

"You may tell such good-for-nothing slander mouths that it would be good for them to learn rightly to distinguish between the spirit and disposition of the devil and the Spirit and nature of Christ before they utter such insipid, ugly words before poor people who know no better than to believe them."

Bettje could tell that the Reformed preacher was trying to goad Father. When it was Jan's turn to churn, she listened to the talk.

"Gellius says you Anabaptists are daily sneaking

secretly into this country sowing your pernicious seeds by night preaching."

"So he accuses me of preaching at night, does he?" Father said with spirit. "What gross wrong Gellius does us with his wicked and bitter words! We cannot let out a peep about the Word of the Lord without such people speaking against us. Would that Gellius omitted such loose talk. Would that he could taste what a true Christian faith is." Father's voice rose. "What a pity that he and his followers walk upon the broad road instead of the narrow road and gate that lead to life!"

"What road is that?" the Reformed preacher asked.

"To lead a penitent and irreproachable life according to the Scriptures. The word of Christ alone is sufficient. We dare not willfully and knowingly deviate one hair's breadth from the Word and example of the Lord."

"But, Menno, don't we all do this?"

Father snorted. "The righteous who fear the Lord are as scarce as grapes in a vineyard carefully gleaned and in which few grapes are left to pluck and use. Tell that to your Gellius Faber, and then let him come to my house himself and defend his views."

But instead of Gellius, the Reformed preacher came the next day with two other preachers and began to argue in front of the family. "Gellius says you sneak into cities and towns, sit behind closed doors, and mislead the simple to make them Anabaptists. He says you should be kept out and silenced lest the simple be misled."

"He is the one who misleads people," Father said.

"Let him come here himself and I'll tell him so."

"Gellius is a minister of the holy Word," one of the other preachers ventured.

"Then why is he full of abuse, false accusations, and secret tyranny?" Father asked. "This does not shut the mouths of the pious but opens them wider. Take heed, all of you. Leave God's holy and precious Word unbroken. Learn to know your own hostile, impure, and bitter heart. Humble yourself under the mighty hand of God, for then you might be helped."

"Gellius says you wrongfully adorn yourself with the sanctity of the church," the third preacher remarked.

"If I should by my teaching gain disciples for myself and not for Christ Jesus, then indeed woe unto my soul," Father said.

"But your doctrine is false," the first preacher cried out.

Father answered quickly. "Judge according to Scripture, with the wide-awake eyes of the soul. By the grace of God you will clearly understand that we, through the grace of God, possess the sure foundation of truth. If you are true preachers, as you pretend, pulverize with the hard hammer of the divine Word the proud, impure hearts, bloodguilty and tyrannical hearts, instead of your unscriptural arguments and your foul slanders—given to you, I know, by Gellius Faber."

"What can one expect from a Munsterite?"

At this attack, Father paced before the men. "We are clear and always have been of the errors of the Munsterites."

"You do not want to be traced back to those of Munster, Amsterdam, and Oude Klooster, where you lost a brother among the three hundred misguided people who gave up their lives."

Bettje heard the words and looked at Jan with disbelief. Father had never mentioned his brother. She had often heard of Aunt Griet, Mother's sister, and Uncle Reyn, Aunt Griet's husband. But why hadn't Father ever talked about his brother?

Father choked up. After a moment, he said quietly, "You rudely refer to the mistake my poor brother made and paid for with his life. My poor brother did no greater wrong than that he wrongly defended his faith with his fists. As for those at Munster, they had, alas, in the past taken up the sword contrary to God's Word. We have to hear about this continually, as if we were one with them in that abomination, although we are wholly innocent in the matter."

The three Reformed preachers murmured their good-byes soon after and left.

"I'll write about this at length someday," Father told Mother.

Other visitors came to the house. One, an earnest young man, told Father, "I heard you preach at a night meeting. I think I'd like to preach, too, but I don't know just how to begin."

"Do not preach on your own account," Father advised at once. "Wait until you are called of the Lord's church. If this takes place, then pastor diligently, preach and teach valiantly."

"The only thing is, what will I live on?" the would-be preacher asked.

"Rent a farm, milk cows, learn a trade, if possible," Father told him. "Do manual labor, and all that which you then fall short of will be provided by pious brethren as necessity requires."

"Ah, if I could only talk like you," the young man sighed.

Father laughed. "A spoken word is but a passing breeze."

"How do I know if I'm called to preach?" the young man asked in parting.

"Servants of the holy Word shall be duly called either by the Lord Himself, or by means of the pious."

Later, Bettje thought over Father's remarks. Father had been called. What had he done before that? She determined to ask him sometime. Both she and Jan were old enough by experience to know more about Father and how he had been called to preach.

One day Bettje heard a man outside call, "Old shoes to mend! Old shoes to mend!" Father invited the man inside.

Mother was delighted and brought the family's shoes out. The shoe mender opened his rucksack and took out tools. "Do you know the Word of God in this household?" he asked in a conversational manner.

Everyone stiffened in alarmed silence. Who was this man?

"I see you do. I can read your faces." Smiling, the shoe mender drew a Bible from his rucksack.

A few comments from Father brought a glow to the shoe mender's face. "You are a learned man?" he asked with respect.

Father chuckled. "I am a poor ignorant man, in comparison with others who are well gifted with learning—less than a fly is to an elephant."

"Are you by chance the one I have heard so much about—the one who preaches at night?"

Father was cautious. "There may be some preachers who work at night because they cannot secure a *Safe Conduct* to face their enemies and defend the doctrine of God, the blessed truth. These preachers conceal themselves in shops and secret places, lest they be torn into pieces by the authorities."

"You have heard of John a Lasco, I suppose," the shoe mender said. "He is a learned man—the pupil of Erasmus. I have been told he bought Erasmus' library."

Father nodded. "This may well be true. It makes me heartily ashamed to write and speak with my dull pen and awkward speech, yet our opinions are all worth equally much before God, for without the command of the holy Scripture nothing pleasing to God can be practiced."

The shoe mender looked both interested and puzzled. "What church are you head of?"

"The church of Christ, which is an assembly of the pious. Although the church is called by different names, yet all who walk according to the Word and will of God are saved by Christ and accepted of God."

The shoe mender gazed at Father. "I want to follow this way."

Later, as one of the brethren, he was the first to warn Father that Countess Anna, influenced by stronger rulers, had consented to expel heretics, especially followers of David Joris and Jan Batenburger.

"They will be corrected on their necks if they do not leave," the shoe mender told the family. (He meant that they would be put to death.)

But, Jan, usually so curious, did not ask what that statement meant. Bettje could see that Jan understood very well—the ax for all heretics.

"John a Lasco is convinced that our brethren should not be dealt with so harshly," the shoe mender went on. "I have heard this in many houses where I stop to mend shoes. But our brethren are being called by your name, Menno, not Anabaptists, but Mennonites."

Father flushed. "Now there will be more misunderstanding by those who will claim I teach to gain disciples rather than to teach God's truth."

"The truth will be victorious," Mother reminded him.

Within a few days the shoe mender's words took on meaning for Bettje and Jan. Taking one of Mother's cheeses to a neighbor, in front of a house they stopped to watch a family load a cart with household goods. Several men walked in and out, examining walls, windows, and doors.

A small child watched with clenched hands.

"What are they doing?" Bettje asked the child.

Two men entered the house, then came out and locked the door with huge bolts.

"Why did they go inside?"

"They put out the hearth fire," the child sobbed.

"But how can your mother do the cooking?"

"She can't. We aren't going to live here anymore."

"Why not?" Bettje asked.

The child rubbed her streaming eyes. "They took our house."

Neighbors came around to watch the family leave. "Anabaptists, you know," they murmured. "Mischief makers, all of them. They practice all kinds of things that lead to sedition and revolt."

Before the family left, Bettje hugged the little

girl. "Trust God," she whispered. "Will you remember that?"

The little girl smiled through her tears, took her place on top of the cart, and the family started on their journey to exile. Who would be the next to go?

At home, Bettje found the answer. Mother was already packing.

"We must leave tonight," Father said, "but first we will attend a final meeting."

That night one of the brethren acted as guide. He took the family to the back door of a shop by the light of a lantern darkened until only a thread of orange light showed through the sliding metal groove.

Inside the shop Bettje heard a rustle. Fifteen or twenty people sat on bales of goods.

"Perhaps we should fight back," someone suggested.

Father objected with his usual vigor. "Christians are not allowed to fight with the sword. Our battle is not a carnal one but a spiritual one. We are armed, not with our own weapons, but with divine ones, the evangelical doctrine—attacked by many but vanquished by none. Avoid every appearance of evil," he urged. "Make a repentant and unblamable life your only weapon."

Someone laid a cloak on the floor. Everyone voluntarily put on it what money he could.

"As the purse bearer for the group," one of the brethren said, "I speak for the others when we say that we want to be sure you have money wherever you go."

A woman wept. "What will we do without you to lead us?"

"I warn all not to place their faith in me nor in any teacher or writer, but only in Christ Jesus. If I cannot teach publicly, I will serve you nevertheless in writing as long as the Lord will permit. I beseech you not to leave these writings idle and hidden, but to send them east, west, north, and south into the hands of all men, that the bright sun of righteousness may shine forth with the power of truth."

The brethren agreed with joy to help send out Father's writings.

"Assist me with your fervent prayers," Father concluded, "so that God will bestow upon me, unworthy and not too capable a man, the fountain of His wisdom that we may stop the mouth of all opponents with the power of a true doctrine."

Father then arranged for someone to take the cow. Bettje did not even shed a tear. Father's safety was far more precious!

Bettje heard him tell someone where the family was going next. "To Cologne," he said in answer to a question. "Archbishop Hermann von Wied is said to be tolerant, even allowing our brethren to live in his district in peace."

One of the brethren offered the use of a wagon and horse. Father decided to wait until dawn before leaving. With a wagon, the family could take more of their possessions. Bettje knew Father hoped to leave unnoticed, but the next morning she saw a neighbor woman already up and watching. It was the woman who had visited Mother when they first came. The woman ran down the road in the rain to the next house. When the family started on their journey, people were staring at them from every house they

passed. Had the neighbor woman informed the authorities? What if they were already in pursuit?

Recent rains had made floodwaters rise. The waves lapped over the pastureland, swallowing the short green grass like a hungry animal. Every year relentless floodwaters crept over the meadows from the sea and often reached the polders, the man-made mounds of earth on which Frieslanders built their houses. The loaded wagon sank deep in the ruts of a muddy cow trail. Then the wagon tilted sharply. Mariken, sitting on top, slid to the marshy ground.

"The wheel's broken," Jan exclaimed.

Dogs barked in the distance. Father glanced at Mother. Bettje read the look. Dogs could mean the captors were near.

"We'll have to abandon the wagon," Father decided. "We must hurry on."

"But, Father," Jan exclaimed, "there isn't even a cow path to follow. There's no road at all."

Under the flooded marsh, there was no sign of path or road. The dogs barked, closer now. Where could the family find safety?

7 THE GATES OF LEEUWARDEN

FOR a moment Bettje thought Father was going to walk right into the marsh. Instead, he picked his way carefully around the edge, with the family following.

"Father, are we going to leave the wagon with everything in it?" Jan called in dismay.

"We must put our trust in God alone," Father answered. "How little we should trouble ourselves about shelter, food, and clothing."

"Somebody will help us," Bettje told Jan. "Maybe that man will."

Ahead, a plump young man ran around and around two black-and-white cows knee-deep in mud. The man flicked the cows with·a slender willow stem and urged them on. The cows tried to pull their legs out of the mudhole. Each time a foreleg came up it went down with a sucking sound into the same spot.

Father stopped to watch. "He'll never get those cows out that way."

"Menno, we must keep going," Mother pleaded.

"But we can't just leave him. Remember the story of the Good Samaritan."

Father talked to the young man, then returned to the wagon and brought back loose boards. With these as stepping-stones, the cows clambered onto solid ground. The young man pranced in delight. Then he stared at Father.

"I hear dogs barking. I know what that means. You be running away, you and your family."

Father stiffened and did not answer.

The young man nodded. "They call me simple-minded hereabouts, but I know a thing or two. My name is Jacob." He kept nodding.

Jan, curious as always, asked, "What do you know?"

"I know that the constables are driving Anabaptists out of the country. My mum says so."

The whole family tensed. Was Father's Good Samaritan act going to endanger them all?

Jacob scratched his leg with the cow stick. "But that is nothing to me. Me and Mum's got these two cows. They give milk. Enough for cheeses. My mum's a good cheese maker. I help her." Jacob blinked. "You saved our cows. We have an attic. You can hide in it. Other people have. Follow me." He led the way around the marsh to a two-story house. On one side the thatched roof had partially collapsed.

"Are we going to stay here?" Jan whispered, aghast.

"It's a shelter," Mother said with a warning glance.

Jacob went inside to talk to his mother. The front door opened wide. Jacob's mother, a blue-eyed vigorous woman, beamed a welcome. At the sound of the dogs barking, she pointed to narrow, ladder-like stairs. "Quick! Up into the attic with you. The officers never look up there. They think because the roof has collapsed there wouldn't be anyone hiding upstairs." She chuckled. "I keep the roof that way on purpose. Now, you don't have to explain anything to me. You brethren all look alike, somehow. I'm not one myself, but I do believe the earth is the Lord's, and I know people are forbidden to offer shelter to you people."

After the family settled down in the tiny storeroom upstairs, not long afterward dogs barked in front of the house. Bettje heard Jacob's mother open the door.

"Have you seen a man and his family come this way?" a man called out.

"Who's going to traipse over the countryside on a wet day like this?" Jacob's mother demanded.

"Yes, it is wet, and we're drenched," the man said. "May we come in and warm ourselves? We won't stay long."

Jacob's mother grunted. "Come in, but mind your promise. We have cows to milk."

From the sounds below, Bettje guessed the men were standing before the fire. She and Jan moved near the top of the stairs to listen. In his eagerness to hear, Jan knocked over a broken crock.

"What was that?" one of the men asked.

Jacob's mother answered quickly, "It must be rats."

"No, no. That was a human noise."

The next moment someone climbed the steps. Bettje clutched Jan. They were caught now. No escape this time! She could hear the dogs growling outside. Heartbeats hammered in her throat. She could think of nothing except that these men would take Father away to be killed.

"Peace be with you!" a man said.

Father bounded out to the top of the stairs. The two men with the dogs turned out to be brethren who had followed Father to offer help. The word of Father's leaving had passed from one brother to another. Within a day the two newcomers had gathered money for Father and more clothes and bedding than the family could use.

"But don't go straight to Cologne," they warned. "Roads and bridges are being watched."

"Then we'll go first to Leeuwarden," Father said. "It is about time for my usual visit."

Mother clasped her hands in joy. "Perhaps we can see your Aunt Griet and Uncle Reyn," she told Bettje and Jan.

The long journey began. The family traveled sometimes by cart, sometimes by boat, and sometimes on foot. One night, with Mother ill again, Father risked stopping at an inn instead of going on to the farmhouse of one of the brethren whom he knew.

The innkeeper rubbed his hands at the sight of Father's coins. "Yes, we have a room. Let me show you."

Bettje had never seen such a cheerful room. A fire burned in the fireplace. The walls glowed with reflected flame. The white hearthstone had been scrubbed until it glistened.

At mealtime, the family sat at the table with other travelers. Two priests talked nearby. One of them was a Swiss.

"I don't know what's worse, the Anabaptists themselves, or the Halfway Anabaptists," the Swiss priest said.

At once Bettje felt a cold chill. Had the priests already discovered who Father was?

"Halfway? What are those?" the other asked.

"They give food, lodging, and aid to these dreadful heretics. They do not report them to the magistrates. Suppose the magistrates plan to lure some Anabaptists in a trap. The Halfways won't help. They claim they have to be home. Or, say, if the Anabaptists escape, the Halfways say they haven't seen anyone, or they complain that the Anabaptists had outrun them. Some of them actually warn Anabaptists that officers are coming."

The room seemed stifling hot to Bettje. She risked a glance at the priests. They paid no attention to Father or the rest of the family.

"Do these Halfways shelter Anabaptists in their homes?"

"No, because they know their houses would be burned, but they do let Anabaptists stay close by, and they don't report them to the authorities."

The other priest shook his head. "Deplorable! And to think the Anabaptists allow themselves to be damned for all eternity. Unbelievable!" He raised a glass. "To the church."

The two priests drank a health and kept on drinking. A little later, one said, "Let us drink to the health of the strangers here tonight."

Father did not respond. One of the priests leaned over. "Friend, I should like to have a little conversation with you about certain things."

Bettje could see Father try to keep from talking. "Words cost necks," he told the priests.

"Join us in a toast to the church," one said, lifting his glass.

Father again did not respond.

The priests, although quite drunk, turned their

attention to him. "Friend, allow yourself to be instructed. We are men of God, and we seek your soul."

The priest's statement was too much for Father. Bettje braced herself. What would Father say?

"Where the church of Christ is, there His Word is preached purely and rightly," Father said.

The priests looked at each other in puzzlement and went on drinking. One scrawled something on a paper and flourished it like a bill under the nose of the other, who read it and poured himself another drink. The note fell to the floor. Father picked it up and glanced at it. His face went ashen.

The two drunken priests did not seem to notice.

"Menno, what is the matter?" Mother asked in a low voice.

"The note says in Latin, 'Here are persons who appear to be Anabaptists. They do not respond to toasts to the church.' "

Mother half rose. "What shall we do?"

"Nothing. We must just wait."

Bettje choked down a few more bites of supper, then gave up. At every movement, every word spoken around her, she twitched with nervous dread. After supper, the family returned to their room. Bettje hunched over, at every step expecting to see Father seized.

A heavy knock sounded on the door. The innkeeper came in, agitated and wringing his hands. "I am sorry, but you cannot stay here."

"Why not?" Father asked.

"I am so sorry—it was all a mistake. You see, I promised others this room."

"But we have paid you already," Father said.

"There have been complaints." The innkeeper rolled his eyes upward.

"Have we been rude or boisterous?" Father asked.

"No, no. It isn't that."

"Have we offended anyone by our actions or words?"

"No, no. You are very quiet people. I saw that at once, but I don't want any trouble. If you'll just go, that's all I ask." The innkeeper's brow glistened with perspiration.

"But what have we done?"

The innkeeper stepped back and glanced down the hall. "I cannot afford to lodge Anabaptists. Even now, someone may have run to get the constable. It means a reward of a guilder, you know."

"Are you sure someone has gone for the constable?"

"I can't say for certain, but it is quite likely. Guilders don't grow on trees, you know."

Father pulled out a guilder. "My wife is ill, but we will be gone by sunrise."

The innkeeper pocketed the coin and left without another word.

At the gates of Leeuwarden, the family lined up with others waiting to be admitted to the city. To avoid close questioning by the keeper of the gates, Father went ahead with Mariken in his arms and Jan beside him. He would wait inside the walls for Bettje and Mother.

Travelers lined up with their bundles, carts, or horses. Bettje and Mother hung back. Soon Father passed through the arched gate with Jan and Mariken.

Then the keeper of the gates called out to the

remaining travelers, "All who desire to enter the city, make haste. The gates are about to close."

At once a bearded, dusty merchant with a cartload of wares protested, "It's only midday. Why are the gates being closed?"

"There are Anabaptists in the city. They are to be seized."

"Is it possible?" Mother whispered to Bettje. "Did someone recognize your father already? I know he's wanted here especially, but he's made trips before safely. But, of course," she added, "we're not the only ones called Anabaptists."

The gatekeeper's announcement passed down the line of travelers.

"Why has the line stopped?" one asked another.

"They're taking prisoners."

The message swept like a cold wind down the line of huddled people.

"What have they done?"

"They're Anabaptists."

Murmurs of disgust rose on all sides. Bettje felt Mother tremble.

"Haven't they sense enough to disguise themselves?" someone asked.

"It wasn't their clothes that gave them away—they had New Testaments on them."

Bettje sighed in relief. It wasn't Father, then. He had no Bible with him. He hardly needed one. Bettje was certain he knew most of the New Testament by heart.

Still, Bettje felt the familiar flutter of heartbeats in her throat when she and Mother came closer to the gates.

She heard the keeper ask a traveler, "Where are you lodging?"

A group of peddlers just ahead talked to each other in angry mutters. "They say there's going to be a rule that no one can rent rooms without going to the officer of the city along with the renter."

"Why is that?"

"You heard the gatekeeper. It's because of those accursed Anabaptists."

The peddlers moved ahead.

"Why have you come to Leeuwarden?" the gatekeeper asked.

"To sell leather," "To sell needles," "To sell spices," came the answers.

They were allowed in. Mother pulled Bettje back. "Not yet," she whispered. "Let's wait."

A man on horseback tapped the long thick roll that hung across his horse's flanks. "What is the delay here? I have perishable goods for the people of Leeuwarden. Are you having the plague?"

At the word *plague*, other travelers murmured and drew back.

The keeper shook his head. "No plague." He crossed himself. "We are to examine all visitors into the city by order of the city council. Have you been rebaptized?"

Mother caught her breath and squeezed Bettje's hand.

"Most assuredly not," the horseman told the keeper.

"Do you adhere to untolerated groups?"

"I adhere to the one true church of the Holy Roman Empire."

"Take the oath and enter."

The horseman murmured the oath and was allowed in.

Other travelers denied being rebaptized, then took the oath and were admitted through the city gates. A woman made an outcry, then choked it off.

"Stay outside," a guard shouted. Two other guards lowered their long pikes.

"Take the oath," the keeper told a man.

"Mother," Bettje said, "we will have to answer all those questions. What will you say?"

Mother's lips tightened. "I don't know yet. Perhaps we can just slip inside with some others."

But the keeper stopped Bettje and Mother. The dreaded question buzzed around them like an angry bee. "Have you been rebaptized?"

"I have been baptized in the true church," Mother said in firm tones.

"Take the oath."

Mother sagged on Bettje's arm. "I cannot," she whispered.

The two guards crossed their pikes. "Stay outside."

"Close the gates," the keeper ordered.

Slowly, the ponderous gates began to close. Bettje stared in terrified disbelief. With no money and no shelter, what would she and Mother do now?

The gates of Leeuwarden swung shut.

8 SHADOW OF THE PAST

FORBIDDEN to enter Leeuwarden, not knowing where to go, Bettje and Mother watched latecomers arrive at the gates, only to turn away bewildered and resentful. Rain fell. In a short time everyone was drenched. From inside the town a church bell rang without ceasing.

"Why do the church bells ring so long?" someone asked in annoyance.

"There has been much rain here," a traveler said. "When there is a bad storm, the bells ring and then the storm passes away."

But the rains did not cease. A group of dairymen drove a herd of cows to the gate and clamored to be let in. Their angry uproar brought a guard to the window of the gate tower.

"The gates are closed," he shouted.

"But it's Friday. These cows are for the cattle market. We were delayed, or we would have been here early this morning. Let us in."

The guard turned to consult someone. After a time the gates opened. Bettje saw a chance to get inside. She grasped Mother's hand, pressed close to a cow's flank, and both she and Mother were swept through the gates as if a wave from the North Sea had propelled them through. The driving rain prevented close questioning by the gatekeeper. Elated by their victory, Bettje felt herself grasped from behind. She twisted away, only to see Father's smiling face. He explained quickly that he had taken Jan and Mariken to the home of two women, Elisabeth Dirks and the widow Hadewijk, where they would all stay.

Elisabeth Dirks, a brisk little woman, hugged Mother and Bettje. "You'll stay here with me. There is plenty of room. Hadewijk is away on a visit. I do hope there won't be a flood," she added. She showed Bettje and Jan her big rowboat, bobbing in the canal in back of the house. "We hold meetings in that boat—but not when it rains." She looked closer. "Why, the water has already reached the top of the back steps."

Other boats bobbed up and down on the pulsating waters.

"They'll have to open the floodgate soon," Elisabeth Dirks said. "But there is no reason why the brethren can't meet. The authorities will be busy helping people." She arranged for the customary notifier to go to various houses and notify the brethren of a meeting at one of the houses. Bettje and Jan agreed to watch the kettles on the fireplace for the later meal of the brethren.

The rain stopped, but at first the floodwaters did not recede. Town officers came to the door. "Is this the house of Elisabeth Dirks and the widow Hadewijk?" one asked.

Bettje nodded.

"Where is Elisabeth Dirks and the widow?"

"I don't know." She listened to one officer explain how Hadewijk's husband had shown sympathy for an executed Anabaptist and had to flee, never to be heard of again. Then the officers discovered the food kettles.

Suddenly, they became hard and demanding. "We know that Anabaptists have been meeting in town. Why is there so much food here, and where are these people?"

"I cannot tell you where my parents are. I do not know," Bettje said.

A call for help from the flooded canal sent the officers outside to assist a neighboring householder retrieve a boat. Then the officers went on to help other people.

Later, after the brethren had slipped in one by one for the meal, Elisabeth Dirks took a firm stand. "If the officers were here once, they'll come again. I think they suspect me anyhow. Menno, you and your family will have to hide somewhere else."

One of the brethren spotted the officers still helping at the flooded boat landings of neighboring people. "They'll soon be here again. What shall we do?"

Elisabeth Dirks ladled out food and handed it out. "Here, take this to the needy." One by one the brethren left.

"Now," Elisabeth said, "the best place for you to hide, Menno, is in the boat—all of you."

Mother gasped.

"Yes," Elisabeth went on, "that will be best. I'll cover you with the leather hides a neighbor gave me." She watched until the officers went into a house. "Follow me."

The family hurried out back and into the boat, lying on the bottom. Elisabeth covered them with hides and tossed in the oars.

The boat bobbed sickeningly. The floodwaters swirled and bumped against the side.

"Whose boat is that?" a voice nearby called out.

"Never mind. It's tied fast. Help me with this one," another answered with impatience.

The boat hit against the landing. Mariken cried out in fear.

"Say! There's someone in that boat. Quick! Catch it."

Before anyone could stir, a boathook landed on the side. The boat was drawn to the dock, the leather hides taken off, and Bettje found herself looking into the faces of the dreaded officers.

Someone shouted, "The floodgate! It's open!"

With a mighty heave, Father wrenched out the boathook and pushed the boat away from Elizabeth Dirks' back steps. The swirling waters shot the boat ahead with terrifying speed and bounced it against the side walls of the canal. A countercurrent tossed the boat back. Before Bettje could catch her breath, the boat plunged through the floodgate and outside the town.

Gradually, the surging waters subsided. Many miles from Leeuwarden the boat nosed into dirt banks. The family, wet and shivering, huddled on the seats. A lone black-and-white cow stood motionless by the canal, pelted by the renewed rain. Bettje sighed, remembering how she and Mother had been helped through Leeuwarden's gates by the market cows. But how could one cow help them here?

She thought of her former dream of a house of

their own, respected by their neighbors. How childish, she thought. Perhaps Mariken was now beginning to think of dreams like that. Such a life would never be, not with Father preaching all over the countryside. Being with Father and Mother, Jan and Mariken, was security enough. No, not enough—God was with them too. How else could Father have escaped with his life so far?

Bettje remembered something Father had once told a timid follower. "Fear not those who take your earthly goods from you. Christ and heaven they cannot take." The memory comforted her, but still she shivered.

A man came over the field to the cow. He patted her flanks. "So there you are! Come on home."

Home! Bettje tried not to envy the cow.

Father hailed the man. "Can you tell me where I can find shelter for my family?"

The man came to the edge of the canal and stared. Was he going to answer anything at all?

"Peace be with you," the dairyman said.

The unexpected greeting used by the brethren warmed Bettje with new hope. The dairyman invited the family to stay at his house. In the next day or so Bettje understood as never before how good it was to be taken in as strangers by other strangers who shared all they had, held together by the common bond of obedience to God's will. The dairyman rounded up other brethren who outfitted the family for the long trip to Cologne. Father memorized a list of names of those who would help them on the way.

Bettje liked Cologne. The city was the largest she

had ever seen. The rented house soon became home-like, and all the occupations of the city fascinated her—the iron workers, locksmiths, weavers at their looms, bellows menders, lantern tinkers, bakers, broom makers, tailors, and workers in iron, leather, and stone.

In the months that followed, Father went on many trips to preach to the brethren. He talked to Mother about meetings in meadows near Fischerswert and Illekhoven, of going by boat to Roermond. He spoke of pious followers of Christ—Metken Vrancken, Lyske Snyer, Jan Neulen. She heard the names of Father's co-workers mentioned many times—Dirk Philips, Adam Pastor, Gillis von Aachen, Leenaert Bouwens.

One day a visitor came to the house in excitement. "What do you know about Albert Hardenburg?" he asked Father.

"Why, he's here in Cologne. He came to help Hermann von Wied, who, as you know, has been very tolerant of the brethren."

"But did you know that Hardenburg and John a Lasco have been writing each other?"

"No, but why shouldn't they?"

"But, Menno, they have been writing about you, but before I tell you about that, just what do you know about Hardenburg?"

"He was educated at the Aduard Monastery near Groningen, and—"

The visitor interrupted. "John a Lasco wrote him that you are here in Cologne 'misleading' many."

Father grunted. "I may have my weaknesses, and do freely acknowledge them, but the Scripture does not mislead."

Bettje could see that the visitor could hardly contain himself, so eager he was to tell what he knew.

"Hardenburg wrote that if one has stupid teachers, he hardly teaches with understanding."

Father winced. For the first time Bettje began to wonder where Father himself had been educated.

The visitor hurried on. "He wrote that those who have left monasteries without study and without correct understanding, or are self-taught, have done much damage to the church. He says you read fanatical books and took the Bible into your own hands without any judgment, and that this has done much harm among the Frisians, Belgians, Saxons, over all Germany, France, Britain, and all surrounding countries so that posterity will not be able to shed sufficient tears on this account. That's what he said," the visitor ended.

Father sighed. "I do not ever want to say or write anything which is contrary to what God has spoken."

"But aren't you going to defend yourself?" the visitor demanded.

"I will write about such things at great length at the proper time," Father said in bidding the visitor good-bye.

Father's visitors fascinated Bettje. One wanted to know what Christ could do for him.

"Do not ask what Christ will do for you, but rather what will you do for Christ," Father told him.

"We know this is the truth," a newcomer said, "but my wife and I are poor and along in years. We can no longer labor and earn."

A young man complained, "We have a house full

of children and cannot earn our bread in other lands."

An old woman was afraid of the new life. "We fear the Lord might not care for us as He did for Abraham."

"We have much property," a young man sighed. "We are young in years and may live long."

"Father and Mother are against it," a woman said.

A wife told Father, "My husband opposes me."

A husband explained, "My wife is against me."

Bettje listened to them, and heard Father say over and over, "Christ promises every necessity if you continue in His way."

When newcomers boasted of family, or wealth, or education, or even of good looks, Father chided, "What good does it do you to strut about with puffed up hearts and stretched out necks? You are like a sparrow perched alone on a housetop."

Some who could not bear to give up their possessions dropped out of the meetings.

"Am I to give up everything?" a man whined.

"To all who agree with the Word," Father explained, "all lawful pure things are pure, such as eating, drinking, clothing, house, home, land, gold, silver, wife, children, goods, fish, flesh, waking, sleeping, speaking, silence, and all things which God has created and given to our support. Use all lawful pure things purely, with thanksgiving and moderation."

"What is it you really teach?" one newcomer asked in curiosity.

"We teach the new life, baptism on confession of

faith, and the Supper in an unblamable church according to the holy gospel of Christ Jesus," Father said.

"Are you against the established church?"

"I am against its dead word," Father retorted. "The power of the living Word leads a man from evil to good and completely renews him."

Bettje noticed that Jan listened to Father, too. Why didn't everyone join the brethren, read Scripture, and uphold a church without spot or wrinkle? How could anyone want to be a poor, misguided Catholic? Couldn't people tell the truth when they heard it?

One day Bettje and Jan went to market for Mother. A tall boy in the neighborhood caught up with them.

"My name is Lubbert," he said. "I've seen you many times, sometimes with your father and sometimes not."

Lubbert had a sly way of talking, as if implying that what Father did was wrong.

"What does your father do?" Lubbert continued blandly.

Even with the tolerance in Cologne Bettje knew enough to be careful. To her relief, today was the day Father was helping a neighbor thatch a roof. She pointed him out to Lubbert. "He's up there thatching." It was good to know that Father did many things like other people.

"That's odd. That's very odd."

Bettje bristled in defense. "Why? What's wrong with thatching roofs?"

"Nothing. Except I know some places your father goes at night."

Bettje sucked in her breath. Was Lubbert a friend or an enemy?

"He preaches in people's attics or empty shops," Lubbert announced.

Jan put his hands on his hips. "Is that all you know about my father? What's so odd about that?"

"I could turn your father in and get a hundred guilders."

Jan's jaw tightened. "Then why don't you?"

Lubbert glanced away. "Because my father has hidden Anabaptists. The authorities could take him, too. That's why I won't tell on your father." He thought a moment, then brightened. "Let's play inquisition."

"What does *inquisition* mean?" Jan asked.

"First you answer questions, and if you don't, then I get to twist your arms until you do. You two pretend to be your father, and I'll be the cross-examiner. Why did you leave the Catholic Church?"

Bettje laughed. "We can't play that game. My father never was a Catholic."

"Oh, yes, he was," Lubbert said. "His name is Menno, son of Simon, and he lived in Witmarsum, and he was a Catholic priest."

Bettje and Jan both cried out, "He was not." Bettje added in scorn, "You don't know what you're talking about."

Lubbert's eyes gleamed with malicious triumph. "Your father was a priest for almost twelve years, and he had to leave the Catholic Church because he didn't believe babies should be baptized. My father told me all about him. Your father is going to have to leave Cologne one of these days, too, because strict

Catholics are taking over pretty soon."

"I don't believe a word you say." Bettje turned to go, her head high. How could Father have possibly been a Catholic priest? He didn't even like Catholics.

9 PUNISHMENT FOR KINDNESS

WAS Father really once a Catholic? The question bothered Bettje.

"If you don't believe your father was once a priest, ask him," Lubbert called after Bettje and Jan. "Better yet, you can ask my father. He's home with a sprained ankle. Ask him yourself."

Bettje knew Jan was tormented, too. Father an ex-priest! Had he worn long robes, with his hair shaved off in a circle? She tried to imagine Father carrying a huge crucifix, lighting candles.

"Do priests believe in God?" Jan whispered.

"Yes, but—"

"Let's go see what Lubbert's father says," Jan urged.

They turned back. Lubbert met them with a knowing grin. "You'll find out the truth," he said. At his house, he called to his father, who hobbled out on crutches.

"These are Menno Simons' children," he explained. "Tell them about his being a priest. They don't believe it."

"Yes, indeed he was a priest at Pingjum and

Witmarsum for almost twelve years, up to 1536," Lubbert's father said. "My sister knew him then, and she said he said masses until the Sunday he openly left the Catholic Church forever."

"Why did he leave?" Bettje asked.

"Because he decided the bread and wine are not the body of Christ, the way the Catholic Church teaches."

The answer confused Bettje more than ever, yet somehow it rang with truth. A new question came to her mind. What would it be like to be a Catholic? What did they do inside their churches?

"You children had better warn your father that strict Catholics will soon take over Cologne. Already there have been signs of persecution," Lubbert's father told them, smiling at their explanations and protests.

At supper, Bettje blurted out the question uppermost in her thinking. "Father, what is a Catholic?" Somehow she did not dare ask a more direct question.

Father put a hand to his beard. "Why? Did someone ask if you were Catholics?"

"Lubbert's father says he knows you, and he told us you used to be a priest, Father. But we said that was false, didn't we, Jan? We said you couldn't possibly have been a priest. You don't even like them."

Father and Mother exchanged glances. As clearly as if she heard them speak, Bettje knew their unspoken question: *Are they old enough to be told?* Mother glanced at Mariken, old enough now to imitate every word she heard.

"Later," she said to Bettje over Mariken's head.

After Mariken was asleep, Bettje asked another question. "Is the Catholic God the same as ours?"

Father's shoulders sagged a little. He did not reply right away, but stood facing the fire.

In bewildered understanding, Bettje gasped, "Father, you *weren't* a priest, were you? Did you really believe bread and wine were the body of Christ?"

"For twelve whole years?" Jan added.

Father took a deep breath. "Longer than that."

Bettje could hardly believe Father's astonishing admission. "But, Father, how could you?"

"*We* don't believe that," Jan added. "Still, I'd like to see what Catholics do in their church."

Father straightened up and said briskly, "Then suppose we go to a Catholic church. You can see for yourselves."

"But, Menno," Mother murmured, "what if they get it into their heads that—"

Father gently interrupted, "This will test their upbringing—and the truth of what I have been preaching night and day for all these years."

The next Sunday, Father took Bettje and Jan to the nearest Catholic church, a buttressed stone building on one of the winding streets not far from the great cathedral of Cologne. A group of people straggled up to a bailiff standing with record book and pen near the entrance. Each person reported to the bailiff, then lined up with the others by the church door.

"Bettje, they don't have any shoes on," Jan whispered in horror. "And what is that sack doing around their necks?"

Bettje studied the group. Did Catholics always

dress in gray? The men and women had bared heads, the women with their hair loose. Bettje could see a white design painted on the front of their gray clothes. A priest came out of the entrance with a cross held aloft. The people followed the priest around the church. Each person held a rod in his left hand, and in the right a lighted candle.

"Is this the way Catholics always dress, Father?"

"No. These people are doing penance."

"What does that mean?" Jan asked.

"They are trying to atone for their sins." Father's voice was tight.

A mother nearby explained to her children, "These are recanters. They've gone through this ritual for six Sundays, and this is the seventh. Then they will have to wear gray clothes for a year and a day, and the only weapon they can carry is a broken bread knife."

Bettje puzzled over the recanters, but once inside, she stared at the elaborate gold candlesticks, the statues, and the gold embroidered vestments on the altar. After the congregation settled down, the recanters filed into church, knelt at the altar, and received absolution by three blows from the priest. The penitent ones remained on their knees throughout the mass.

The priest, with shaven, uncovered head, in a robe reaching the floor, folded his hands and celebrated the mass. Bettje wondered at the many movements of the priest. He lifted up a chalice, muttering unintelligible words. The people murmured at intervals.

Afterward, Father, Bettje, and Jan sat on the stone ledge of a fountain near the cathedral.

"Don't you have the same God as the Catholics, Father?"

He did not answer directly. "Water, bread, and wine do not make a Christian."

"But aren't the priests Christians?"

Father became excited. "The priests are prophets, but not of God; they preach, but not out of the Lord's mouth. They preach for a handful of barley and a slice of bread." Father warmed up. "A priest buys a hundred wafers for a nickel, nods to it, worships it, prays to it, eats it. He kneels and burns incense before blocks of stone and wood. They point the poor people to legends, histories, fables, holy days, images, holy water, tapers, palms, confessionals, pilgrimages, masses, matins, and vespers. They teach that a piece of bread and a sip of wine turn into the actual body and blood of Christ. Do you think Christ was there, Bettje?"

"No," Bettje admitted.

"Common sense teaches us that Christ cannot be taken into one's mouth nor digested by the stomach," Father said. "Priests are after fat salaries and a lazy life. Thousands of poor souls have been deceived and are deceived still. I was a priest once, but by the grace of God, I and many others belong to the true church of Christ."

On the way home, Mariken came to meet them, sobbing.

Father scooped her up in his arms. "What's the matter?"

Sobs answered him.

"Mariken, tell me. How can I help you if you don't tell me what the trouble is?"

Mariken pulled her tiny apron over her face and

sobbed anew. Father tugged at the apron with one hand.

"They said I was going to burn." Mariken clung to Father's neck.

Father peeled her hands away. "Who said?"

"Some children down the street. They said I was going to burn for eternity in hell because I'm not baptized. And they asked me my name, and when I told them, they laughed and said I couldn't even have a name, because I'm not baptized. A priest has to baptize me. Father, I don't want to die. Those children said they'd chase me to the fountain and duck me until I drowned because I'm an Anabaptist, they said." Mariken brooded for many days and would not be comforted.

One day Bettje and Jan came home from market laden with food. Mother met them with a worried expression. "Is Mariken with you?"

"No, Mother. Why?"

"She's gone. She was just outside the door playing, and the next thing I knew, she was gone. Will you look for her?"

Bettje and Jan started out. "You go toward the river and I'll go by the cathedral," Bettje suggested. "She can't have gone very far."

Jan hurried off. Bettje heard chanting not far away and hurried toward the sounds. People had gathered in the street, necks craned toward a procession. Bettje glimpsed Mariken trying to push through the tightly knit onlookers.

"Mariken!" Bettje called.

Her little sister turned and waved her to come.

"It's just a procession," Bettje said when she caught up with Mariken. "Father wouldn't want us to stay and watch."

"Wait," Mariken pleaded. "It's a parade. Listen to the men playing on those funny long things."

Two men on horseback, wearing hoods and cloaks, their hose half red and half white, blew on trumpets from which tapering banners fluttered. Behind them on a high cart drawn by horses a young woman stood with her arms bound behind her. She looked into the distance with a faint smile.

The sight chilled Bettje. She had never seen such a sight in her life, but she knew what it meant. A strange dread burned through her body. "Mariken, we have to go home."

"No, please. Look at the pretty lady. Why is she standing in that cart like that?"

Tears smarted under Bettje's eyelids. "Come away, come away!"

"No. I want to see the pretty lady some more."

The onlookers in eager excitement pressed forward and jostled Bettje and Mariken closer.

"I would gladly draw the wood with my own horses," a man called out.

"The Anabaptists' piety is nothing but outward show," another said. "Fire will prove it."

A priest ran up to the slow-moving cart and held a crucifix before the young woman's face. "Kiss your Lord and God."

"This is not my God," the young woman said. "It is only a wooden image."

"My lady, have you considered well the things which my lords proposed to you?"

"I abide by what I have said," the young woman replied.

Some of the women spectators wept and called out,

"Recant!" The young woman paid no attention but began to sing a hymn. Bettje dragged the protesting Mariken away. At supper Mariken began to prattle about the pretty lady. Bettje wished Father were home.

"She stood on a cart and sang, like this." Mariken put her hands behind her back, looked up at the ceiling, and began to sing.

Mother gasped. "Where were you?"

"By the cathedral," Mariken said. "There was a big cart, and the pretty lady stood there and sang. Some mean men tried to hit her, and the others said, 'No, let her sing.' "

"And then?" Mother's voice tensed.

"Then Bettje made me come home."

Later, Father came home, pale and sorrowful. "Did you hear about the martyr?" he whispered to Mother. "Oh! what noble wheat they destroyed today!"

"It's true, then, that strict Catholics are taking over Cologne?" Mother asked.

Father nodded.

"When I grow up, I'm going to sing on a wagon like that with everybody watching me," Mariken said.

Father caught her to him but did not chide her. "We'll go to Wismar next," Father said. "It's Lutheran and a free city."

The two years of security in Cologne were over. Father could no longer be protected. Strict Catholics had taken over the district government. All along the city was Catholic, indeed the seat of an archbishop. The safest plan was for Father to go on ahead, leaving secretly at night, with Mother and the children to follow.

Soon after Father left, Mother became ill. On the

advice of one of the brethren, Bettje and Jan approached a homeowner just outside Cologne.

"Our mother is sick. We need a place to stay—a room will do. We have money," Bettje explained.

"You say your father is not with you now?" The man hesitated, then agreed. "I'll let you have one room—just one room, mind you. You understand that you have to report to the authorities now that you are moving, don't you?"

Bettje admitted that she knew.

"Be sure to report as soon as your mother is better." The man pursed his lips. "In these times, it pays to be careful."

In a short time, the family packed what possessions each could carry and started out on the trip to Wismar. Bettje saw that she had forgotten her clogs for rainy weather. She ran back to the house. Two officers came to the door and bolted it with wooden bars before she could enter. The men tacked a sign on the door. After the men left, Bettje mingled with the curious neighbors to see what the sign said. There was much scratching of heads. No one could read, and Bettje did not disclose the fact that she could. The words were clear:

"Confiscated by order of the city council"

The whole neighborhood knew somehow that the house was being confiscated, and discussed the matter among themselves.

"Why was it confiscated?" Bettje asked, dreading to hear the answer she suspected.

"He rented a room to Anabaptists," was the answer. "Wherever these Anabaptists go, death and destruction follow."

Bettje was forced to agree.

10 A PAINFUL TRUTH

IN the following days of travel, escorted from village to village by brethren, and sheltered each night at someone's home, Bettje kept thinking about what happened to people who helped Father. *Death and destruction*. The words haunted her.

"Of course we know the risk," one of their hosts cheerfully admitted when Bettje blurted the question, "but the authorities can't capture everyone who helps your father. No matter how many spies and traitors there are—and we know there are some who even call themselves brethren—God's will is greater than man's. Hasn't your father taught you that faith is stronger than death?"

Bettje nodded. Sleepy from the long ride that day in a borrowed wagon, she tried to understand this faith. Each evening of the long trip one of the brethren joyfully sheltered Father's family. Which of them would be caught later on and punished by death, or at least by having their house confiscated or burned to the ground? She dreaded being introduced as Menno Simons' daughter.

One evening, after a day of travel, Bettje and Jan

went to the town well for water. A cluster of women talked in agitated tones.

"Is it true you are being banished even when you have lived quietly and without offense to anyone?" a woman asked in disbelief.

"Yes, they are already closing our houses against us," another answered.

A third drew up a pail of water and smiled over her shoulder. "They haven't caught Menno, though."

"Ssssh! Don't mention our leader by name," someone warned.

Jan nudged Bettje. "Don't tell them who we are."

So he felt the same dread she did! Bettje felt comforted.

The women went on talking. "Are you going to have your new baby baptized?" one asked another.

"Of course not, and we've already been told to choose baptism or leave the city," the new mother said. "Just think, we've lived here all our lives—my parents and grandparents, too."

"No sacrifice is too great for the treasure we have now," another woman said with a smile.

Bettje heard and understood the faith that was stronger than death.

"How were we discovered?" someone asked. "Was there a spy at the preaching when Menno was here?"

"No. Someone reported the church path through the meadows."

A strong, new voice broke in. "Did you know that the Hollanders have been draining marshy land in Oberland? There are whole villages of no one except brethren—Bardeyn, Thierbach, Schmauch, Liebenau, to name a few. Why can't we go north as a group? We could have a self-contained community."

A gasp of comprehension greeted her words. "Yes —yes! A community all our own! That will be the answer to our prayers."

The new hope of these women so soon to be exiled excited Bettje. A sudden, inner conviction rose in her. In the future there would be new settlements where the brethren could live and work, without persecution and worshiping in a church that Father dreamed of—one without spot or wrinkle.

On the way back to their host's house with wooden buckets of water, Bettje and Jan had to walk around two men in a heated argument.

"But you are on the council," one man said.

"I refuse to sit in on this meeting."

"But it is to condemn an Anabaptist."

"I will not condemn such a pious man."

"You will fall in disfavor with our gracious lord and prince."

"I would rather be in disfavor with the prince than with God," the other retorted.

"You will not be allowed to practice your profession here any longer," the first man said.

"I am quite aware of that."

"Have you perchance joined the brotherhood?" The first man clutched the other by the shoulder.

"That you will have to find out for yourself." The second man wrenched himself free and strode away.

Bettje gazed at the determined back of the man who refused to condemn a pious Anabaptist. How long would this man escape punishment?

In the marketplace of another town, Bettje and Jan joined a large crowd who watched a constable question one of the brethren.

"Aren't you Anabaptists bound to tell the truth?" the constable sneered.

"Yes."

"Then tell me who your accomplices are."

"To accuse our neighbor is not the truth; Christ does not teach that. Besides, the man you want has already left town."

"Impossible!" the constable exclaimed. "No one can leave here so secretly no one knows about it."

"But he has."

"Doesn't he know all bridges and passes are guarded?"

"He left at night."

"But the bridges and passes are even more closely guarded then," the constable raged.

The onlookers tittered, and the constable hurried off.

Later, when the family was together again, this time on a rented farm near Lubeck, Father listened to Jan describe the incident. No, he was not the man who escaped that night. "How much time the authorities spend threshing empty straw," he remarked.

Father soon began night preaching in the Schleswig-Holstein area. In the months that followed, Bettje and Jan became notifiers, going from house to house to notify the brethren of meetings in fields, attics, or storerooms, but always in secret. During that time, Father had important meetings with his co-workers, Dirk Philips, Leenaert Bouwens, and Gillis von Aachen. In spite of widespread persecution, Father hoped for eventual public meetings.

"Before I left Cologne," Bettje heard him tell a group, "I asked the preachers of Bonn to hold a

105

public meeting with *Safe Conduct.* I also wrote twice to those of Emden and once to those of Wesel on the same condition. My request was refused by those of Emden and Bonn, and as for the preachers of Wesel, they wished that the hangman would take care of the public meeting."

Father and his co-workers covered great distances in their planned preaching. Bettje learned that three members of Illekhoven had been put to death, and two years later, news came that Claes Jansz Brongers, a man who had been host to Father, had been beheaded.

"But he wasn't even one of the brethren," Mother gasped. "But," she admitted, "I know he had your father's books, and of course he had attended meetings for years—but this—only six weeks after Menno was there!"

Bettje shuddered at the news, but when news of Elisabeth Dirks' execution came, she prayed in desperation for understanding. She tried not to dwell on the idea that haunted her—death and destruction following Father's preaching—but busied herself with Jan in teaching Mariken how to read and write. Mariken, too, seemed haunted by some fear. One day, it burst forth.

"Catholics tell lies, don't they?" Mariken asked Bettje and Jan.

Bettje remembered the incident in Cologne when Catholic children had told Mariken she would burn for eternity for not being baptized. Bettje chose her words carefully. "They tell what they have been taught." She looked questioningly at Jan. What would Mariken do if she learned that Father had been a Catholic most of his life?

106

"Why doesn't Father let us be baptized?"

"Because you're still a child," Jan told her. "Father says infant baptism is not ordained of God. It's a human invention, he says."

Mariken was not satisfied. "Why aren't we baptized, Father?" she asked one night at supper.

"Because Christ Jesus commanded His church to baptize believers on confession of faith," Father told her.

Mariken's face worked with perplexity. Then she brightened. "I confess my faith. Can I be baptized now?"

"Little ones must wait according to God's Word until they can understand the holy gospel of grace."

Mariken's hidden fear came out. "But what if they die before that?"

"They die under the promise of God. They are saved, holy and pure, pleasing to God, under the covenant, and in His church."

Later, Mariken cornered Bettje and Jan. "You're both old enough. Why aren't you baptized?"

The question caught Bettje unprepared. It was true. She and Jan were now old enough. What better preparation could anyone have than with Father, who believed his own children should be the first to follow the faith?

"Don't you believe Father's faith?" Mariken pursued.

"Of course."

"Then why aren't you baptized? Are you and Jan halfway people?"

Jan's usually pale face flushed. "Father is so busy with other people. Besides," he added, as if inspired, "we'll wait for you, won't we, Bettje?"

"You will?" Mariken's thoughtful face lit up.

Bettje agreed, and determined to listen to every word Father said about baptism. It had been just a word for so long. Now she must find out the meaning behind it.

"When will Bettje and Jan be baptized, Menno?" someone asked Father one day.

"When they are ready to confess their faith," Father said.

In astonishment Bettje wondered what Father had been thinking about Jan and her all this time. She and her brother had worked many months as notifier for the brethren, yet had never professed their faith. What must Father have thought? Had he been waiting patiently all this time for them to volunteer their profession of faith? She determined to learn more about the gospel of grace and help Jan and Mariken, too.

Another visitor argued with Father about baptism. "Menno, Luther says that faith is dormant and hidden in children, even as in a believing person who is asleep."

Father answered, "I may be an unlearned man, but I am not satisfied with the doctrine of Martin Luther. We do not read in Scripture that the apostles baptized a single believer while he was asleep. Why then baptize children before their sleeping faith awakens? The Lord neither taught nor commanded it."

The visitor, a newcomer still not sure of the new faith, began, "But the Catholic Church—"

Father interrupted. "They baptize before the thing which is represented by baptism, namely, faith, is found. This is as logical as to place the cart before the horse, to sow before we have plowed, to build before we have the lumber at hand, or to seal a letter before it is written."

"But the Bible—"

"Infant baptism is nowhere commanded nor implied in the divine Word. We proclaim it to be idolatrous, useless, and empty, and we do this, not only with words, but also at the cost of our lives." Father took a deep breath and continued, "Although infants have neither faith nor baptism, don't think they are therefore lost. Oh, no! they are saved, alone by grace through Christ Jesus. Christ has promised the kingdom to small children without baptism."

Later, still another newcomer tried to argue. "Menno, how can you go against the church with its hundreds of years of doctrine?" He added slyly, "Can't God work faith in children?"

Father tugged at his beard. "We are not speaking of the power of God. He does not at all times do all that He could or might do. We speak only of the precept of the Scriptures. Since infants do not have the ability to hear, they cannot believe, and they cannot be born again. Reason teaches us that they cannot understand the Word of God. The regenerating Word must first be heard and believed with a sincere heart."

"But," the visitor argued stubbornly, "Jesus said, 'Suffer the little children.' "

"Christ did not say a single word about infant baptism. He commanded that believers be baptized and not infants. All thinking men must admit that infant baptism, although, alas, practiced by nearly the whole world and maintained by force, is nothing but a ceremony of those who do not follow Christ's teaching. Our Catholic friends baptize such things as little unconscious children and bells, which God has not commanded to be baptized. They do not baptize those whom God has commanded to be baptized, namely, those who believe."

Other people were troubled about a second baptism. "Do we have to be baptized again?" they asked.

"If you are a genuine Christian born of God," Father challenged them, "why do you draw back from baptism, which is the least that God has commanded you? Who is so unbelieving and disobedient that he refuses God a handful of water? As long as your minds are not renewed and you are not of the same mind with Christ, are not washed in the inner man with clean water from the living fountain of God, you may well say, 'What good can water do?' As long as you are earthly minded, the whole ocean is not enough to cleanse you." Father marked his words with his forefinger. "For where there is no renewing, regenerating faith leading to obedience, there is no baptism."

Still, many newcomers hesitated. Second baptism meant torture and death for hundreds who had professed their faith.

"God's work is not keeping a dead letter, nor is it the sounding of bells and organs and singing," Father explained over and over. "It is a heavenly power, a vital moving of the Holy Ghost, which warms the hearts and minds of believers; encourages, rouses, stirs, and makes one joyful and happy in God."

"I am sure God would be displeased if I were baptized again," someone ventured.

"Do you suppose that the new birth consists in

nothing but to be plunged into the water, or in the saying, 'I baptize thee in the name of the Father, and of the Son, and of the Holy Ghost'? No. The new birth is the heavenly, living, and quickening power of God in our hearts. Water baptism avails nothing so long as we are not inwardly renewed, regenerated, and baptized in our hearts with the heavenly fire. The new birth is an inward change. The inner man is washed, not the body. We bind ourselves, however, by the outward sign of the covenant in water," Father said.

"Ah," someone exclaimed in triumph, "then you insist on rites."

Father almost lost his patience. "Baptism is secondary. I know many say they were baptized once in the name of God and that sufficed. But I say if they feared God with all their hearts, they would be forced to conclude that they had not been baptized in the name of God but contrary to it." He added, "The Word is plain. Thou shalt love the Lord thy God, abide in the word of Christ, and lead a holy life before the whole world."

Bettje, Jan, and Mariken listened to Father's explanations to many different people. Then from somewhere Mariken learned that Father had been a Catholic priest. One day when the whole family went to market, a drunken priest reeled from an inn and swayed down the street ahead of them.

"You were never like that when you were a priest, were you, Father?" Mariken asked in utmost confidence.

Father's cheekbones flamed above his long beard. "Yes, I was. I thought I was a Christian, yet nothing I did was done without sin. I was a leader in all

111

manner of folly—empty talk, vanity, playing cards, drinking. . . ."

Mariken pulled back. Her face showed utter shock. Bettje saw that Father, in telling Mariken the truth, regretted his youthful folly probably more than he ever had in his life.

11 REFUGEES FROM ENGLAND

MARIKEN stared at Father in utter disbelief. "Drunk? You mean you were *drunk?* Father, how could you?"

Bettje and Jan exchanged grins. Mariken sounded just like them several years before when they had first found out about Father's life as a Catholic priest.

"Do I get drunk now, Mariken?" Father asked.

"Of course not."

"Now, Mariken, what do you think made me change my way of living?"

Father's question challenged Mariken. "God wanted you to," she said at last.

"Yes," Father agreed, "and in order to show me, He opened the eyes of my heart. So, Mariken, do not dwell on my past weakness, but look at Christ, His Word, Spirit, and example."

Mariken lowered her head in thought. "Did the authorities try to catch you when you were a priest?"

Bettje could see that Mariken had touched a sensitive spot.

Father sighed. "While I served the world, I received its reward. All men spoke well of me, but when I turned away from the proud ungodliness of this world and sought God, I found everywhere the opposite. Before, as a priest, I was honored; now I was hated. Once I was everyone's friend; now I became an enemy. I had been considered wise; now people considered me a fool. They thought I had been pious, but now wicked; then a Christian, now a heretic." He added in a low voice, "So cruelly am I hated that those who show me love, favor, and mercy must look for prison and death."

Young as she was, Mariken determined to be worthy of baptism. In her zeal, she spurred on both Bettje and Jan. The day came when all three approached Father with their request for baptism. He hugged them, his eyes bright with unshed tears.

"If I love the salvation of my neighbors, many of whom I have never seen," he told Mother, "how much more should I have at heart the salvation of the dear children whom God has given us?"

"I wish Griet could have been baptized like this," Mother said after the baptism of Bettje, Jan, and Mariken. Aunt Griet had written how troubled she was because she had been baptized by Douwe Schoenmaker, a revolutionary preacher. Bettje had overheard how Aunt Griet had asked first Father, then Leenaert Bouwens, one of Father's co-workers, to baptize her again. Both had refused.

"She must not follow her own head and imagine it to be the Spirit and Scripture. We must follow Him and not He us," Father said.

Somehow these words brought a full understanding to Bettje. God's way was not the world's way. When He awakened the inner spirit of people, they were endowed with more than human strength. That was how they could endure persecution and death, strong and steadfast to the end. That was why people sheltered Father at great risk to themselves—not for Father's sake but for the sake of following God.

Father's secret preaching continued. In between his travels, he wrote a long reply to Gellius Faber, so full of what he wanted to write that his pen was hardly ever behind his ear. During the winter of 1553, the family moved to Wismar. Once more the children were warned to keep their house hidden from prying eyes.

One December day a messenger hurried to the house. "I must speak to your father." The messenger stamped his feet and blew on his hands.

When Father came out of his study, pen in hand, the messenger burst out with his news. "There is a shipload of people locked in the ice out in the harbor. They tried to land in Denmark, but weren't allowed to; so they came here."

"Who are they?" Father asked.

"Refugees from England," the messenger said.

"The city fathers will take care of them," Mother murmured in concern.

"But Wismar is a Lutheran city," the messenger explained. "These people are Zwinglians. That's why they couldn't land in Denmark."

A number of the brethren were notified of the need.

"Do we dare risk showing ourselves to help them over the ice?" one questioned. "We're barely tolerated here in Wismar ourselves."

"If we can help them without antagonizing the city government," others suggested, "then we should."

Father chided the cautious view. "A true Christian

will help even his most bitter enemy," he reminded the group.

The brethren gathered up food supplies and sleds. Bettje, Jan, and Mariken struggled across the iced-in harbor with the others, heads bowed against the icy blasts, and boarded the ship.

"It's deserted," someone exclaimed.

Voices sounded from the hold. The brethren found the refugees huddled in prayer. They looked up, astonished and grateful, when the brethren introduced themselves. Then came the astonishing news: These were not really Englishmen, but part of John a Lasco's group. John a Lasco had been forced to leave Emden during 1548, and until Queen Mary began persecution of Protestants, he had pastored his refugee flock in London. The leader of the ice-bound ship in Wismar harbor was Hermes Backereel.

"They'll need money," the brethren whispered among themselves. Quickly a discreet collection of twenty-four thalers was offered.

Hermes Backereel waved the money away. "We do not need money, but would there be any work our people could do?"

The brethren offered what they could. Someone offered to keep the children over the winter.

Hermes Backereel, the leader, stiffened. "No, no. That will never do."

"What do you mean?" the brethren asked in astonishment.

"These are children of John a Lasco," Hermes Backereel announced in a haughty tone. "John a Lasco, of course, is a nobleman. I'm sure you can appreciate the difficulty."

"But they will have to be sheltered somewhere."

"John a Lasco deals with lords, princes, and high personages. Don't you understand?" Hermes Backereel's irritation grated on Bettje. "It would cause a scandal if his children stayed in a place not in accord with their rank."

"I see we have not met with the true, plain, and humble pilgrims of Jesus Christ," Father said later. "Brotherly love is very thin with them."

A few days later, Bettje was with a group of brethren. Hermes Backereel came with a request. "I would like a discussion about your principles, but since I am a clergyman, I would have to dispute with another clergyman." He cleared his throat. "I understand your Menno Simons is here in Wismar. I would like to debate with him."

When Bettje told Father, he paced the floor of his study in irritation. "Hermes has a slippery tongue," he snapped. "He hopes to find a splinter about me to magnify into a big beam and tie it on my back." Then he told Bettje and Jan how Hermes had found out who Mariken was and had tried to get her to tell where the family lived.

Father sent word to the brethren. "Tell Hermes and his followers that I'll talk with them on the following condition—that they will tell no one where the discussion takes place."

The messenger returned with the promise. "They gave their hand on it," he said.

On the day of the discussion, the house was filled with people on both sides. Father talked about the true cross of Christians.

Hermes bristled. "Menno, you wish to make my doctrines suspect among your party."

"I had not so much as thought of that," Father

said, astonished. "Very well," he added, "I suppose you would like to discuss the question of the incarnation first."

"Yes."

Everyone in the room settled down to listen. Bettje, Jan, and Mariken huddled close to the doorway of another room and listened to Hermes talk on and on.

When he was through, Father said, "Dear Hermes, look out what you say, for behold all these absurdities follow from your belief." Father enumerated eight, counting them off on his fingers.

One of Hermes' group, Jacob Michiels, asked, "Can you prove your statements from Scripture?"

"Ask that question of Hermes," Father said, "since it is his faith and doctrine."

Jacob Michiels looked down and was silent. Father asked Hermes three times to prove his point from Scripture. When Hermes did not reply, Father said, "Dear sirs, are we to treat the Word of the Lord thus? What a pity! When you thought that it was my doctrine, you asked for Scripture, but when you discovered that it is Hermes' position, you have Scripture enough. O friend," Father went on, "repent and be ashamed before God, for you do not treat His Word as becomes a true Christian."

Later Hermes found his tongue. "I will scatter these absurdities as the wind scatters the dust."

"Dear Hermes," Father said softly, "do not speak so proudly. It does not become a Christian."

After more discussion, Bettje, Jan, and Mariken helped serve a simple meal to the visitors. The talk never ceased. Hermes Backereel looked more and more dejected. At parting time, Father laughed a little. "Dear Hermes, you will have to learn a great deal more before you try to defend your cause."

A few weeks later, the house filled again with people ready to listen to further discussion. Hermes had with him a small man named Martin Micron. Whispers and excited glances told Bettje that Martin Micron must be an important member of Hermes' group. She, together with Jan and Mariken, once again listened carefully.

Father began, "I hear that your name is Martin Micron. You are unknown to me, and I have never in all my days heard a word about you before you came here. But I understand that you have made a reputation in London by your speaking and that you have published some things also, as I here. Therefore, I request that if you hear more powerful truths and firmer foundation in this our discussion than you have heard or learned before this, you seek not your own fame and honor but the praise and honor of the Lord."

Micron folded his arms. "Menno, I admonish you the same."

"I am here for that very purpose," Father replied, "and I have suffered for many years because I wished to know the truth and to follow it."

In the discussion, Micron repeated one statement four or five times, and tried to prove a point by reading from the Bible more than an hour. He read in such a monotonous voice that Mariken fell asleep.

Then Micron made an accusation. "Menno, you accused me of seeking my own praise and honor by my writing and speaking in London."

"Why, I had never thought of it," Father exclaimed. "I did not even know you."

Micron appealed to his own group as witnesses. "Did you not hear this?"

They all agreed that was what they had heard.

"Is there no fear of God before your eyes?" Father asked. "There are now ten of you, all of whom answer as he wants. If there were ten thousand more besides you, you would still not tell the truth in this matter."

The men argued on and on. Bettje could see that Father was both irritated and yet excited by the talk. At one point he muttered, "Fairy tales," in reply to one of Micron's arguments. In an aside to some of the brethren, he said, "Dear me, if we poor folk were to abuse the Scriptures one-twentieth part as much as they do and would pull the wool over the eyes of simple people as does Micron, then how they would turn up their noses at us."

Micron argued further. "God is the cause of Adam's corruption."

"Why?" people questioned.

"Because God said, 'In the day that thou eatest thereof thou shalt surely die.' "

"Do I hear you say that God was the cause of Adam's sin?" Father asked.

"No, I did not say that, Menno."

"Oh, Micron, what absurdities you advance! What a weak, unscriptural position you assert and maintain!"

For a long time Micron said nothing. Then he asked, "Do you believe that Mary was a human being?"

Father grew reckless and answered, "She certainly was not a cow, was she?"

Bettje smiled to herself, remembering how years

ago she had startled Father by naming the family cow *Mary*. From the discreet coughs and clearing of throats from a number of people at the same time, everyone enjoyed Father's retort, but Bettje knew he would apologize in writing for his thoughtless, almost reckless, reply.

When Micron proposed another discussion, Father readily agreed. Bettje was not surprised. Father loved to talk.

"Did you know that Gellius Faber has issued a publication against us?" Father asked at the next meeting. "Have you read it?"

"Yes," Micron replied.

"Well, how do you like it?"

"It is an excellent tract. I have also let our brethren read it."

"Ah, Martin," Father exclaimed, "do you extol that wicked shame so full of shameful falsehood in which the Word and ordinances of the Lord are so grievously mutilated?" He went on, "John a Lasco and you see eye to eye in this doctrine."

Martin Micron asked to read the assertions of a Lasco. When he studied them, he said, "It is written a bit obscurely."

"Obscurely," Father said, "yes, wickedly."

The heated discussion went on for some time. When everyone started out—Bettje and Mother escorted the guests to the forepart of the house—a noisy argument broke forth, even though Father had not come out with them. Jan and Mariken listened.

"They're so noisy, everybody on the street will know where we live," Mariken whispered.

But it was not these meetings that betrayed the family's secret dwelling, Bettje learned later. Hermes

122

Backereel had not kept his promise. Not long afterward, Father learned that where he lived was known even on the streets of Emden.

It was time to move again.

"That is as clear as the midday sun," Father said.

12 FRUIT OF THE DESERT

WHERE would they go? Where could they go? Where *should* they go? Over and over the question came up. Father had writing to do, books to be published and distributed, his preaching to continue over wide areas. Then there were disputes among church members to be settled through discussions with his co-workers.

Father began to have sleepless nights. Bettje heard him many times pacing the house at night. The soft slap-slap of his slippers was somehow more frightening than an attack on the house.

"What's Father doing?" Mariken whispered to Bettje one night. "I watched him, and all he does is walk up and down."

"He's worried. He has so many problems on his mind."

"But doesn't God take care of people's problems?" Mariken asked.

"You have to do your best first," Bettje said. "God

doesn't just stand by ready to do man's work for him."

"No," Mariken agreed. "He just gives you the strength to do it."

"I've heard Father say many times how dearly he must pay for wanting true worship—he receives oppression, trouble, sleeplessness, fear, anxiety. . . ."

"This is the sleepless part," Mariken said, going to the door and listening to Father's shuffling through the house.

Jan tiptoed in. "What are you two doing up in the middle of the night?" he whispered.

"It's Father. He can't sleep again. This must be the fourth night at least," Bettje explained.

The shuffling in the other room stopped. Bettje heard a groan, then a thump.

"He's fallen down!" Jan exclaimed.

"He's probably asleep on the floor," Bettje added. "Let's put him to bed—but don't wake Mother."

Jan lit a candle and put it on the table by the hearth fire. The three children bent over Father. One leg lay crumpled under him.

"He's not asleep—he's hurt!" Mariken said.

In the shadows, one side of Father's face looked curiously drawn. It took all the strength all three could muster to help Father to bed. Bettje knew Father was ill, in addition to the injury his leg had suffered when he fell. She sent Jan and Mariken to get a few hours' more sleep and sat by Father's bed until daybreak.

One of the brethren came to warn the family to move as soon as possible. Persecution of all Anabaptists had started again.

"Tell him we can't move now," Bettje told Jan, "not with Father this way."

Father must have understood that persecution was starting. "Not even a hog house," he kept muttering.

"What do you mean by 'hog house'?" Bettje asked when he was able to sit up a few days later.

"We are not allowed a hog house in which to live safely under heaven," Father said.

One side of Father's body was partially paralyzed. When he discovered he would have to use a crutch at times to get around, instead of despairing, he made light of his ailment. "Just call me 'the cripple,' " he kept saying.

The problem of where to move to next stayed with the family. Then one of the brethren made a suggestion. "Menno, you know about Baron von Ahlefeldt's estate. You know the baron let persecuted brethren live there as early as 1543."

The family listened carefully. Baron Bartholomew von Ahlefeldt had the highest respect for the steadfastness of the brethren. His estate lay between Hamburg and Lubeck, about seven miles from Hamburg, three miles from Lubeck, and nearly a mile from Oldesloe.

"But the king of Denmark has put pressure on the baron," Father objected.

"The baron has never changed his policy, Menno."

But Father did not want to leave Wismar.

Father's visitor was patient. "What's the longest you have lived in one place since your call?"

With a rueful smile, Father admitted, "Scarcely more than half a year."

"Your printer is already there," the visitor went

on. "I understand the baron has built him a print shop. What better arrangement can there be?"

Bettje ventured a joke. "It would at least be a hog house, Father."

Father smiled, and from that moment planned the move in his usual vigorous way.

On the trip to Baron von Ahlefeldt's estate, Bettje noticed two passersby looking at Father, who rode beside Mother on a two-wheeled cart.

"What do you think happened to that man?" she heard one say.

"A punishment by God," the other answered at once. "A stroke like lightning that twisted half his face."

The man's human judgment made Bettje reflect on the mysterious renewing power God granted His followers when they woke inwardly. Father's illness had not shaken his faith. Mother's long years of ill health had not weakened her beliefs. Bettje tested her own inner convictions. Here they all were, once more fleeing for a new place of safety. What about her old dream of security—one house for a lifetime, as many people had, and yes, a cow? She smiled involuntarily. Would she trade the faith of the brethren for the world's judgments?

"No," she said aloud, and walked faster.

"What did you say, Bettje?" Mariken asked, catching up.

"I wouldn't trade."

Mariken glanced at some villagers watching the family pass through. "I wouldn't either."

Jan seemed to understand, too, and echoed, "Nor I."

Mother turned. "What are you children talking about?"

127

All three smiled and waved, then walked on ahead of the cart.

Not long afterward, the family settled on Wustenfelde as their choice of village on the estate of the baron. They had hardly moved in when a servant from the baron's own house came to Father. "It is with exceeding regret that my master begs to inform you that because of circumstances beyond his control, he must order you and your family to leave here before sundown."

"But we have hardly arrived," Father said, pen in hand. "What have we done?"

"The emperor's orders," the servant murmured. "You have heard and understood the message?"

Father nodded. The family stared at each other. Where could they go now?

Bettje was the first to move. She started the familiar chore of packing up, rolling the bedding first. Another servant galloped up to the open door.

"Did you receive the message?"

"Yes. Before sundown. Tell the baron we shall comply," Father said.

The servant grinned and leaned down from his horse. "You don't have to go."

Everyone sat down in weariness and stared at the servant.

"What is this mockery?" Bettje blurted.

"My master was just following orders," the servant informed them with another grin. "He was ordered to tell you to leave. He has faithfully communicated the order to you. He has no intention of carrying out the order, and never did have, even from the beginning, over ten years ago, when he welcomed the first refugees of your brotherhood."

"You mean we can stay?" Mariken asked.

"You are most welcome here," the servant assured her, and rode off with a wave of his cap.

Within a short time, in a peace and quiet the family had never known before, Father settled down to revise many of his earlier writings, and to translate them from Dutch into the dialect spoken in this region.

One day a group of travelers came to the house and asked to see Father.

Bettje tiptoed to the study. Father was fumbling among the papers on his desk.

"Bettje, where is my pen? Did one of you children take it?"

"It's behind your ear, Father."

"Oh." Father reached up for the pen and began to write at a furious pace, grunting a little as he always did when his pen could not keep up with his thoughts. Bettje backed away. She did not dare interrupt him when he was writing. Father always tossed off interruptions with a shrug of his broad shoulders and a series of amiable grunts, never looking up.

Bettje went out to explain. The visitors were there, crowding every corner, with such expectant hope in their tired faces that Bettje knew this time she would have to let Father know. These people needed help—the help that Father could give in guiding them to a true understanding of God's promise to His people and what He expected of them.

"Father," she said with determination, "there are some people here who need you."

Father did not look up.

"They need your help," Bettje said.

Father grunted in an amiable way, but did not quit writing.

"Father, you said once, 'If but a single, troubled, shaken, doubting soul might be helped along—' "

Father jumped up. "I shall count that dearer than all else under heaven," he finished. "Who is it, Bettje? Who is troubled?"

Bettje led him to the door. Father surveyed the roomful of people with his head on one side, as if astonished, Bettje thought—or as if listening.

The group of dusty travelers rose and surged forward.

"You are Menno Simons," a gray-bearded man stated rather than asked. "We have traveled many days to find you. We have come to learn about the true church."

Mother interrupted hospitably. "It's so late in the day. You must have something to eat first, and then rest. Tomorrow will be soon enough."

The gray-bearded man shook his head. "I speak for all of us. We are hungry, it is true, but for the Word of God. We have been misled for so long."

Father took a deep breath. "For other foundation can no man lay than that is laid," he began the familiar motto.

In the doorway of another room, Bettje stood with Jan and Mariken and all three formed the remaining words on their lips, "Which is Jesus Christ."

The tired faces of the visitors glowed as if with an inner light. Bettje sensed Father's calling as

never before. No matter what difficulties or dis-
sensions among the various groups of brethren in
the future, when Father spoke, the church of Christ
came to life through him without spot or wrinkle.

Father's enthusiasm was contagious. The visitors
sat alert on benches and floor, eager and questing.

Father gave his whole strength in his eagerness
to share the promise of the Scripture. As for his
preaching, at the rate he was going, Bettje could
see it would continue the rest of the day and all
night, too.

THE END

Louise A. Vernon was born in Coquille, Oregon. Her grandparents crossed the plains in covered wagons as young children.

She earned her BA degree from Willamette University, Salem, Oregon, and studied music at Cincinnati Conservatory. She took advanced studies in music in Los Angeles, after which she turned to Christian journalism. Following three years of special study in creative writing, she began her successful series of religious-heritage juveniles. She teaches creative writing in the San Jose public school district.

Mrs. Vernon recreates for children the stories of Reformation times and acquaints them with great figures in church history. She has traveled throughout England and Germany researching firsthand the settings for her stories. In each book she places a child on the scene with the historical character and involves him in an exciting plot.

The National Association of Christian Schools, representing more than 8,000 Christian educators, honored *Ink on His Fingers,* as one of the two best children's books with a Christian message released in 1972.

Mrs. Vernon is author of *Peter and the Pilgrims* (early America), *Strangers in the Land* (the Huguenots), *The Secret Church* (the Anabaptists), *The Bible Smuggler* (William Tyndale), *Key to the Prison* (George Fox and the Quakers), *Night Preacher* (Menno Simons and the Anabaptists), *The Beggars' Bible* (John Wycliffe), *Ink on His Fingers* (Johann Gutenberg), *Doctor in Rags* (Paracelsus and the Hutterites), *Thunderstorm in Church* (Martin Luther), *A Heart Strangely Warmed* (John Wesley), *The Man Who Laid the Egg* (Erasmus), and *The King's Book* (the King James version of the Bible).